SURVIVE

THE HUNTSMAN CLAN BOOK THREE

ROSE ALEXANDER

Editing: Muddy Waters Editing

Cover: Black Glitter Press

❀ Created with Vellum

DEDICATION

Mike, you are my rock.

CHAPTER ONE

LIA

Snap awake, but everything is still black. I try to move but my hands are tied behind my back and my legs are tied to a chair. I scream, but no one responds. My heart is racing. The last thing I remember is looking in the limo for the driver.

There's a musty smell I can't quite place. Even though it's pitch black, I can make out bare concrete walls and a single bulb hanging from a chain above me. It feels as if we are underground. Maybe in a basement. Kylah is pacing in the back of my head, agitated.

"We can't shift," she growls, my agitation growing to match hers.

"Let me try," I offer, needing to do something.

"It's a waste of time," she huffs, still pacing.

I try to calm my mind and focus on pulling her forward. I can feel her right under my skin, but I can't seem to grasp ahold of her. I growl in frustration.

A bright light flickers on, chasing away the darkness and causing me to wince at the intensity. A man wearing a black ski mask steps into view.

"You can scream all you want little princess, no one can hear you," he says, his voice deep and curt. "I will make a lot of money for delivering you."

He walks forward carrying a syringe. Kneeling in front of me, he pulls up the sleeve of my shirt exposing my arm. I thrash about, but he has a firm hold on me. He jabs the needle in, and I feel an instant burning as the liquid invades my tissue, spreading out. He silently gets up and turns the light back off and exits the room, leaving me alone with my racing thoughts. What am I going to do? How can I get out of here?

My mind becomes muddied. I try to reach out to my mates, but I can't feel them. What does that mean? Are they ok? Did something happen to them too?

My legs have gone numb. Sitting in the dark, I have no way to know how long I've been tied to this chair. I've given up screaming, my throat sore from my efforts. My thoughts are so jumbled, and my heart is breaking with the loss of my mates. I can see why the lion at school stayed feral if this is what he experienced.

Sometime later the overhead light flickers on. I squeeze my eyes shut and wince from the pain of the bright light after being in the dark for so long.

"I smell a lion, a tiger, and a bear," Kylah says, waking up from her spot in the back of my head.

"Oh my," I reply sarcastically.

"Wait, we know the bear!" Kylah perks up. *"He's getting closer."*

"Who is it?" I ask. I try to open my eyes a crack, but only see two men in front of me wearing masks.

"I don't know, but he's familiar," she huffs, sounding frustrated. *"Everything is muted right now."*

The men are talking quietly in the doorway, but even with my enhanced hearing I can't make out what they are saying. One guy takes off while the other approaches me. A crash shakes the ceiling, causing the remaining man to move with more urgency.

"Sorry princess, just following orders," he says before pulling out another syringe.

"Please don't," I beg, struggling against the ropes that bind me to the chair.

He grabs my arm but before the needle can puncture my arm, he's ripped away. Looking up, I see a tall, brown, grizzly bear pinning the masked man to the ground.

The pinned man shifts, but before he can finish the bear lets out a deafening roar, stopping the other shifter's progress. He bashes his head, knocking him out.

The bear vibrates and shrinks in size, shifting back to human. It's the alpha!

"I've found her; come help me tie them up," I hear the alpha call. He's the bear Kylah felt.

"There are more bears," she says sniffing the air.

"Amelia, are you ok?" Alpha asks as he unties me from the chair.

I nod my head yes, barely holding back the tears that threaten to stream down my face. Who knows what would have happened to me if they hadn't found me so quickly?

"How did you find me?" I ask, coming out in a hoarse whisper.

"One of my bears saw you being taken in the house and reported it," he explains as he tries to help me stand.

My legs are asleep so I would have crumbled to the floor if not for his strong arms holding me up. My head is swimming as he scoops me up in his arms and carries me out the door and up a set of stairs.

"Tie those cats up now!" he bellows. "Then take them to the confinement room at the compound."

"How long have I been gone for?" I ask.

"Only a day. It took time to get everything together. We had no idea what we would run into. Thankfully, it was only those two buffoons," he answers gently, though his eyes are fierce with anger brewing just under the surface.

"My family…" Crap, I can't imagine the worry. I still feel weak and I can't reach them. "I think they drugged me."

"Your family drugged you?" he asks, confusion flashes across his face.

"No, sorry. I think those cats drugged me. I'm just worried about my family," I try to explain my thoughts feeling a bit jumbled. "I can't feel them."

"We'll have a healer look at you when we get to the compound." I open my mouth to protest. I just want my family, but he quickly continues, "Your family is there with the cats you brought," I let out a sigh of relief. I can feel as the adrenaline dissipates from my system and the exhaustion of the event takes over. My lids close and I let the safety of the darkness take me without a fight.

I don't know how long I had drifted through the darkness, but I felt as it slowly left me, and I found myself lying in a bed. An overwhelming scent of bleach seemed to force its way suddenly in my nose while a scratchy sheet brushed against my legs as I shifted and slowly opened my eyes. The first thing I notice is the steady beeping of the monitors placed strategically around the head of my bed. As my eyes adjust to the fluorescent lights above, the smiling face of my mom takes shape, followed by each of my guys: Kenton, Dom, Reid, Spence, Vance, and my other family, Jack, and Rachael. My heart soars at the sight of all of them.

"Amelia," my mom gasps when she sees my eyes open. She runs forward and pulls me into a bear hug.

"Mom," I gasp and the dam breaks. Tears stream down my face. I'm so relieved to be back with my family.

"I still can't feel our mates," Kylah growls, causing me to frown.

I glance around, closer, and everyone from my cat family is frowning.

"Lia, we can't feel you or Kylah anymore," Kenton struggles to keep his voice calm.

"It's like you were dead," Vance meets my eyes with his haunted ones.

"I'm here and I can still hear Kylah, but I couldn't shift," I explain, still not feeling like I can.

"How can we not feel you?" Kenton asks, pain dulling his eyes.

"They drugged me with something. I became weak and couldn't feel any of you anymore," I explain, my voice warbling.

Carter, the bear pack's healer, interrupts when he comes in to check on me. He checks the machine that is monitoring my vital signs and frowns.

"We assumed they used monkshood on you, but you're not recovering like you should be," he says his brow furrowed in concern.

"What's that mean?" my heart races.

"We don't know yet," Carter gives me a sad look and walks back out the door.

Jack follows him, pulling his phone out. Why is everyone so quiet? What aren't they telling me?

"Not even poison can keep us from shifting," Dom says before leaving the room.

"Where's everyone going?" I panic.

"Jack is calling Queen Adrielle and Dom will tell him about the shifting thing," Spence grabs my hand and rubs his thumb in a circle on the back of it.

"She will not make us come back before Christmas, will she?" I look around, but everyone's faces are grim.

"Probably, but maybe your family can come too?" Rachael offers, giving me a small smile.

"That's not fair to them. The pack is important for holidays," my face drops, and a single tear slides down my face.

This just proved to me I can't have both worlds. I have to cut ties to keep them safe. What if they go after my family next time to get to me?

"Stop worrying. We will work something out," my mom says tenderly. Her face is set in an expression of firm resolve. If she believes it, then maybe I should too?

"We are stronger than this. Stop being such a coward," Kylah hisses.

"Fine. Let's get out of here, and see what the assholes who took us know," I say back to her, sitting up straighter. She's right, this is not the time to be weak.

"Help me up. I want to know what they were planning," I tell Spence who is standing closest to me.

He looks around the room concerned, obviously not wanting me to know something.

"What?" I ask, as I swing my weak legs over the side of the bed.

"I don't think you want to see what they are doing, Trouble," Kenton finally answers.

"Listen to him, Kitten," Dom sighs as he walks in the room.

"I hope they're making them bleed," I growl.

I pull off the sticky pads connected to my chest, then rip the IV out of my arm before standing up; my legs briefly wobble before I catch my balance and straighten. Holding the hospital gown closed behind me I walk to the door.

I open the door and leave the room before anyone thinks to stop me. Slowly I walk down the hallway of the medical ward until it opens into the gathering hall. I haven't been here since my shifting ceremony. A small weight forms in my chest, remembering the night everything changed. It occurs to me I don't have a clue where the holding cells are; it wasn't something they shared with the children.

"Alpha!" I yell at the top of my lungs, knowing his shifter hearing will pick it up no matter where in the building he is.

Mr. Henderson, one of his betas, comes into the hall glaring at me. "Just because you're one of the Huntsman, doesn't mean you have rights here, cub," he growls at me.

His words bring back the feeling I had when my friends wouldn't talk to me after my first shift. I can still remember the stares of shock and how everyone treated me like I was a pariah. I'll be damned if I let them intimidate me now though.

I stand up straighter and meet his eyes, staring him down. "I'm not a cub, and you better think before you speak again. I didn't call for you. I called for the alpha. Where is he?"

His eyes dart to the floor, my dominance winning, though I can tell it pisses him off further. "How's a little kitten like you going to make me tell you?" Vitriol drips from his words.

"I may be young, but you know I'm dominate. I'm sure I can figure it out," I spit back.

His body stiffens at my response. He opens his mouth to reply but stops himself when a large hand lands on his shoulder. "You should be smarter than to poke her, Bill. She would eat you for dinner," Alpha says, amusement lighting up his eyes. "I'm glad you are awake, Amelia. Maybe you can force these cats to talk," he sighs and gestures for me to follow him.

I follow behind him, silently wondering how he expects me to do anything. I feel a tingle in my back and whip my head around to find Jack stalking up silently behind me.

"Connect with Kylah, tell her you want these bastards to be human. She will walk you through the rest," he whispers softly by my ear when he catches up.

I nod my head, taking a deep breath, and prepare for

what's about to happen. We reach a large metal door I've never seen before. Alpha knocks twice and two bears open it, letting us pass through, before closing it behind us.

Inside is a large room with several cells all have reinforced steel bars separating them. The outside walls and floors are all solid concrete. I can't imagine any shifters escaping from here.

In one cell to the right is the lion, and the tiger is in the cell to the left. I can see why the bears need help. Both are in their animal forms, stalking the length of their confines.

"We need them forced back into their human forms," Alpha explains. "Kenton tried but wasn't able to command them."

"How do I do this?" I ask, taking a deep breath and reminding myself I'm more dominate the Kenton. "Wait why can't you do it, Alpha? You forced me," I ask, remembering how he forced my first shift back to human.

He chuckles. "Because you were brand new, I could force you to shift back. I can force a shift in a bear, but not an older cat. If they were in their human forms, I could have prevented a shift, but they shifted while I wasn't in here."

"Remember what I said," Jack puts his hand on my shoulder and starts whispering in my ear.

"Kylah, did you hear what Jack said?" I ask her tentatively. Kylah gets up and stalks closer to the surface.

"We can do this. Just relax and let me slip under the surface," she smiles, which is creepy on her panther face.

I relax and feel her moving just under the surface then feel the power radiating off of me. All the shifters in human form drop to their knees, a look of terror crosses over Alpha's face briefly before he schools himself into a neutral expression. Man, I must be more powerful than I thought.

"Tell the lion to shift, now!" Kylah commands.

I step in front of the lion's cell and boom, "Shift!"

His body contorts and I can feel his bones snapping and reforming. I've never felt another's shift before and it's oddly exhilarating. I keep my focus pointed at the lion until a naked human is lying in front of me with a pained expression on his face.

"*Ok, pull back, please,*" I ask Kylah, the power rush is going to my head. I like it a little too much.

"*Are you sure?*" she asks.

"*Yes, if he switches, we can do it again,*" I assure her.

The shifters around me stand up. I hear a gasp from Jack when his eyes land on the lion, now in his human form. I study the man. He's a tall dark-haired man with muscles only intense weightlifting can cause. As he turns and I get a glimpse of his face, I realize this man was with Queen Rani at Thanksgiving. What the hell is going on?

"Lia, be careful. I have to call Queen Adrielle back," he says, barely a whisper.

He pulls his phone out and walks back towards the door. I'm dying to know what the conversation is. I look back and forth between Jack and Alpha, trying to decide if I should follow him or not.

"Go, he won't be able to shift again for a bit after that," he reassures me.

I take off after Jack and meet him at the metal door. He raises an eyebrow at me but doesn't stop me. Once the bears let us through the door, he dials the phone and places it on speakerphone so I can hear better.

"What is it Jack?" my grandmother's voice floods through the phone, full of concern.

"Lia forced the lion to shift. It's one of the lion queen's betas. We have enemies inside the castle," he tells her through gritted teeth. I gasp, bringing my hand to cover my open mouth.

"I suspected as much but couldn't do anything without

proof. Keep him alive, we are leaving now," she says before hanging up the phone.

"My grandmother is coming here?" I ask, eyes widening.

"She is concerned for your well-being, and this adds another layer to her visit. We can no longer trust Kenton's mother," his eyes meet mine, pleading with me to listen.

"You think she's a part of the Radicals?" I ask, hoping maybe the beta was acting on his own.

"I think she IS the Radicals," Jack replies, before knocking on the steel door.

"Wait! What? She's already a queen, why would she try…" I ask confused. My mind can't wrap my mind around this.

"I don't know, Lia. But that is her first beta in there. Unless this has nothing to do with the Radicals… But either way she had something to do with you being kidnapped. She's not to be trusted," he growls in frustration.

"Who's not to be trusted?" Kenton asks. We were so preoccupied with our conversation we did not hear the guys walk up.

"Your mother," I meet his eyes daring him to challenge me.

"That's ridiculous! She might be cold, but she would never hurt her people," Kenton growls back, his eyes turning dark.

Jack shrugs and we walk through the door to see if they've gotten the lion to talk. As soon as Kenton's eyes land on the man his jaw ticks, and he clenches his fists.

"You have two seconds to explain why you kidnapped my mate," he bellows, everyone but me flinches.

"You have no power, little prince. Why should I?" he sneers back.

"Because I will rip you to shreds if you don't answer him," I reply deadly calm as Kylah slips to the surface.

"You're in no position to threaten me. Do you know who I am?" he stands up, trying to put on a false bravado.

"I know my mother wouldn't publicly back someone who attacked royalty. Would she Maxwell?" Kenton raises his eyebrow at the man.

Maxwell's face blanches. "But I was, she said…" he stumbles over his words, visibly shook up.

The tiger on the other side of the room, who is now a naked man, yells, "Shut up, idiot. These kids don't know how to make us talk yet!"

"Good thing Queen Adrielle is on her way then," Jack says, the corners of his mouth rising in a wicked smile.

"Wait, there's no need for the panther queen to get involved. I'm sure you could contact Queen Rani and clear up this big misunderstanding," the tiger says, wringing his hands together.

"How could my mother clear up you kidnapping my mate?" Kenton lunges at the bars in front of the nervous tiger.

"I mean… I don't… Fuck…" he plops down, hitting the side of his head with his hand.

"Come on, we need to get out of here," Kenton grabs my arm and starts dragging me towards the door.

"Stop," I tell him, and thankfully he listens. "Never grab me like that again. I would have followed if you would have just asked me," I stare him down.

His eyes fill with guilt. "Crap, sorry, Lia. I just can't believe my mother… I mean she's not a very loving woman, but this?"

"All will be revealed once Queen Adrielle arrives," Jack puts his arm across Kenton's shoulders and leads him through the now open door.

We make our way back to the main hall where my parents are sitting talking to Carter. They go silent as soon as they see us approach. By the looks on their faces, there isn't good news.

"What's going on?" I ask, trying to keep my nerves in check.

"We ran a tox screen on your blood and it came back. They injected you with Tacca Chantrieri," he explains, not meeting my eyes.

"Are you positive?" Jack asks, his teeth clenched together.

"Yes," Carter replies still staring at the table.

"What's taca whatever you said?" I ask not understanding the reaction.

"Cat whiskers, or devil flower," Jack says, though the name clarifies nothing for me. The rest of the cats hiss when they hear it though.

"Explain it to me like I'm dumb," I tell him.

"It's a potent toxin to cat shifters. It can kill us in large enough doses. In smaller doses, it knocks us out. But it doesn't explain why we can't feel you or why you can't shift," Jack replies, giving Carter a pensive look.

"Maybe they mutated the strain," Reid suggests, a grim look on his face.

"How long does it take to get rid of this toxin?" I ask, looking around.

"Weeks, maybe months," Rachael whispers. "That they gave it to you at all is a death sentence for them."

"There is an antidote," Carter speaks up, my heart jumps at those words. Maybe he can fix me! "But I don't know how to get any."

"Well, what is it?" Jack asks him, growing impatient.

"Orthosiphon, according to my reading," Carter replies, giving him a nervous glance before looking down.

"Jack, calm down you're scaring him," I place my hand on his arm.

"Are you an omega?" he asks Carter, much gentler.

Carter nods his head yes, refusing to raise his eyes.

"I'm sorry. I didn't realize. I will try to be calmer when you're around," he sighs, plopping on the chair next to my dad. "I'll tell the queen the new development and maybe they have something on hand."

I didn't realize he was one, but once Jack asked, it makes sense. Omegas are bottom of the pack, least dominant. In bear society we protect them, keep them safe. It makes sense a healer would be one. I wonder how they are treated in the Huntsman clan. I've heard wolves don't treat theirs well.

He gets out his phone and walks off to call her straight away. My mind is spinning, and I can't focus on the conversation. This doesn't sound like the work of the Radicals. Something is nagging at the back of my mind.

Kenton's phone rings and his eyes darken when he looks at the caller id.

"Mother," he answers, biting the word out. I move close to see what she says.

"Kenton, my dear boy. I just heard Amelia is missing. It's not safe for you to be there. You need to return home," she says, her voice dripping with fake concern.

"You would expect me to leave my mate, when she's missing?" he asks, his eyes wide with shock. "You know my bond won't allow that."

"I'm sure it won't be a problem. Can you even feel her? If she isn't conscious, your bond shouldn't be an issue," she says flippantly.

"How did you hear Lia was missing again? And how would you know if she is conscious or not?" he asks, his eyes full of suspicion.

"Oh, someone reported it to the queens earlier. I don't keep track of those trivialities. Besides, if someone could kidnap her there is no way she's lucid," she attempts to brush the subject off.

"I'm not leaving my mate. As queen, even you can't order something so deplorable," Kenton growls at her.

"Nonsense. If she were really your mate, she would be a lion," she hisses back at him.

"You know that's rubbish. Goodbye, Mother," he hangs up, his face a mask of fury.

Kenton stomps off. I get up to follow him, but Spence catches my arm.

"Let him walk this off. He might say something he regrets," watching his friend leave with a knowing look.

"No, we need to hash this out now," I stare Spence down.

He throws his hands up and shrugs. "Just be warned, when he's like this he can be nasty," he says, giving me a worried look.

"I can handle anything he can throw at me," I say before

rushing out the door and catching up to Kenton. "We need to talk."

"Not now Lia," he growls.

"Yes, now!" I growl back. "Let's go outside."

"Fine," he relents and follows me to the front door.

We walk around to the side of the building and I lean against the wall, sliding down until I'm sitting on the ground. Kenton paces back and forth in front of me, his hands clenched in fists at his sides.

"I can't believe she...." he starts then cuts off and grabs his head. "I can't do this right now. When I get back, ok?" his eyes plead with me.

"Ok, when you get back," I agree.

He runs off, leaving me sitting there watching him go. I slowly push back to my feet and join the others in the gathering hall. I sit down next to my mom and she rubs small circles on my back, which have an instant calming effect on me. I rest my head on the table and fight to keep my eyes open. My eyelids are so heavy, I lose the battle.

A gentle shaking rouses me. My neck is stiff, and the lighting in the room has changed since I rested my eyes. How long was I asleep for? My grandmother is standing above me with a concerned look on her face.

"We need to get back to the medical ward," she whispers.

"Why," I mutter, still not awake.

"I think it's best child," She bunches her brow at me.

"But I feel fine." I shrug before standing up.

Everyone is looking at me with concern. I look down at my body and it's covered with black fur, so naturally, I scream. What the hell is going on with me?

"I don't know if our antidote will work. This is unlike anything I've ever seen before, but I will question those who took you as soon as we try to get you treated," she says, her lips forming a thin line as we walk back to the medical ward.

"Why am I covered in fur?" I ask, feeling the panic rising in my chest.

"You tried to shift in your sleep," Reid explains in a calm voice. "We think the drug that is keeping you from shifting is wearing off, so you're caught in a half shift."

My tail flicks in agitation. Wait, I have a fucking tail? I turn around in circles trying to look at my backside, then realize how stupid I must look and stop. I guess at least no one can see me blush under this fur.

We return to the room I first woke up in, and I climb on the bed, glad to be lying down. I'm still so tired and overwhelmed. The adults have their heads together talking about something, but I'm too tired to care.

"Go back to sleep," Spence says before kissing my forehead.

I close my eyes, thinking I'll just let them rest for a minute.

CHAPTER THREE

JACK

Carter is fidgeting; too many dominant shifters make him nervous, and the room is full of them, save for Lia's adoptive parents.

"Give her the antidote," Queen Adrielle tells him gently.

"Yes, Your Highness," he almost whispers before scurrying over to Lia. Who knew bears could scurry?

As he prepares the injection, Vance's phone rings. He looks down at the caller id and growls, sending it to voicemail.

"Krissy is trying to call me," he rolls his eyes as his phone rings again.

"Looks like she really wants to talk to you." I raise an eyebrow at him, wondering if he will bother with the vapid girl.

He sends it to voicemail, but it rings again.

"What!" he yells into the phone.

As he listens to what she has to say, his face grows pale.

"Stop!" he screams at Carter.

"What? I've already given it to her?" Carter says, looking like he will piss himself.

"Fuck! Krissy, I'm putting you on speakerphone so you can tell everyone what you just told me," he says into the phone then presses a button. "Go ahead."

"Ok, so, I should have called sooner but I'm scared of Queen Rani. But I don't want Lia to get hurt, so I really need to let you guys know what I know, you know?" she rambles.

"Get to the point," I growl, a pit forming in my stomach.

"So, Queen Rani doesn't think it's right for her son to be with a panther, so she wants to get rid of Lia or at least break their bond. So, she hired Kelly and Amy to scare her off, hoping she would leave and go back to the bears. When that didn't work, she told me to monitor her, but I didn't really want to, so I tried to just send her stupid reports. But she said she has it taken care of now because she sent someone to break Lia's bond and it was perfect because the antidote to the poison would force her to sleep forever," Krissy says really fast. My mind takes a moment to process what she just said.

"So, you're telling me, we just put my sister in a coma?" I bellow, causing Carter to scramble out of the room.

Kenton rushes forward. "Lia wake up," he shakes her shoulder. "Come on, Trouble, can you hear me?"

She doesn't respond, as he continues to shake her, only stopping as her body shifts back to human. All traces of her half-shift now gone.

"I don't know. I just was trying to call before anything happened, but I was too late," she says then hangs up.

"That evil bitch!" Queen Adrielle screams, her eyes on fire. Her panther is prowling close to the surface.

I wince, fighting the urge to kneel to the ground. Looking around, Rachael and I are the only ones left on our feet, and I'm losing the battle. I sink to my knees, hoping she will regain control of her emotions soon.

She grabs her phone and makes a call. "Calyope, we need to know exactly what Rani is doing. My granddaughter is in a coma, her beta put her there and some vapid girl claims Rani ordered her to get Lia away from her son," her voice sounds calm and collected, yet dominance is still radiating off of her in waves.

"Thank you; yes, Rachael is safe," she says to the leopard queen as her panther finally recedes.

The moment I can move, my arms instantly go around Rachael's waist and land on the area where our baby is growing underneath. I need to send her home to keep her safe, but I can't leave my sister like this. I want to growl in frustration, but I'm trying to hold it together. I have too many people looking to me for strength right now.

"Tell my mom, I won't leave Lia. She needs us to help her," Rachael speaks up. So much for that idea, I could no sooner change her mind than I could tell the sun not to rise.

The queen steps out of the room and continues her conversation, while we all stare at the sleeping Lia. Kenton needs to come back so he can see what his mother is capable of. I don't know how we will take the queen down, but it will happen.

"Someone needs to go get Kenton; he needs to know what's happened," I tell the guys standing around Lia.

None of them move; none of us want to leave her side. I hold in a growl and try to rein in my irritation.

"Fine, Reid, you go," I stare him down.

He sighs and slowly exits the room. I'm not prepared for the lion prince's reaction. I know he will probably lose it, especially after the call he had that made him storm off. That boy has a temper.

I feel helpless, much like I did when I lost my brother. I can't lose her too. There has to be something we can do, someone who can help. Jace is prowling under my skin, wanting to run. I will have to check with the alpha on where it's safe for us all to let our cats out soon. Except for Rachael. She can't shift again until after the baby is born.

Standing around here is doing nothing to help Lia. I can't take it anymore. Suppressing a growl, I bolt out of the room, heading back to where I last saw the bear alpha.

"I thought you were supposed to be the level-headed one," Queen Adrielle calls out from behind me.

I whip around and look at her. She's put together, but the pain is clear in her eyes. I take a deep breath and try to push Jace back. He's too far forward, making me too impulsive.

"I can't stand around and do nothing. She's just lying there and staring at her will fix nothing," I explain, pain leaking through in my voice; even though I'm trying to hold it back.

"What would you have us do?" she asks, arching an eyebrow inquisitively at me.

"First, I was going to find the alpha here and get permission for the cats to run off some steam. With all the emotions in that room it's a ticking time bomb. I haven't thought any further past that," I reply, realizing I don't really have a plan at all.

"That's a good first step. Clear your mind and wear your cat out," she smiles at me.

"What do you have planned?" I ask, not expecting an honest answer.

"It's been a long time since anyone has been brave enough to address me so casually," she laughs. "I will interrogate the cats that are being held and decide their fate then I'll figure out what comes next."

"I hope they suffer," I mutter under my breath before I can stop myself.

"Don't worry, son. They will. I don't care whose cats they

are. They wronged my family, so they will pay." Her face grows dark and a shudder runs down my back. She may be small, but she is fierce.

I nod my agreement before continuing on to find the bear alpha.

CHAPTER FOUR

KENTON

*A*fter hearing my mother's smug voice, I feel like I will explode. Running out of the dining area, I bolt outside. I wish Lia wouldn't have tried to stop me. I can't talk to her right now. As soon as she agrees to talk to me later, I take off into the woods, strip off my clothes, and let my lion out. I don't even stop and think about the consequences of shifting in someone else's territory.

Percy, my lion, takes control, and we run blindly until I'm panting so hard, I flop on my side. I know my mother is a cold woman, but surely, she's not capable of this. Something nags at me. Why would she assume Lia wasn't conscious? I shift back and start jogging back the way I came from.

Wood, Reid's panther, pops in my head. "Where the hell are you?" he growls.

"We're heading back," Percy answers for me.

"Hurry!" he yells, agitation coating his words.

I pick up the pace and nearly run into Reid when I get closer to the compound. One look at his face and my heart sinks.

"What happened?" I demand. I slow to a walk and he falls in beside me.

"It not good, brother. Lia is in a coma," he explains. "Krissy…"

I cut him off. "My mother did this didn't she?" I growl, venom dripping from my words.

"We believe so. How did you know?" Reid gives me a weary side eye.

"When she called, she assumed Lia was unconscious," I sigh, trying to hold it together.

"Krissy called Vance and explained Queen Rani put Amy and Kelly up to all of their crap and ordered her to spy on Lia. Coupled with the fact her beta is in a cell at the compound, the evidence is pretty damning. According to Krissy, the poison was made so the antidote would make her sleep forever," Reid explains, his voice strangely devoid of all feeling.

"Fuck!" I roar, punching the nearest tree, causing my knuckles to scrape and bleed.

"What are we going to do? We can't lose her?" I ask, my voice suddenly small.

"Kill her," Percy growls. *"She's not our mother if she hurts our mate."*

Reid's eyes grow wide. Obviously, Percy felt like sharing that thought. Though I have to say, I agree with my lion. She's attacked my mate, and she doesn't deserve to live. When we reach where I left my clothes strewn on the ground, we pause so I can get dressed before continuing on our walk back.

I try to collect myself as we enter the compound. The walk back wasn't nearly long enough. As we turn the corner and head down the hallway to Lia's room, my heart pounds in my chest. I don't know if I can handle seeing her like this. I reach up and tug on a lock of my hair, trying to distract myself from the anxiety building in my chest.

I stop in front of her door and straighten my back. I have to be strong for the others. They've always looked to me as the most dominant of our little family and I can't let them down now.

Slowly, I reach for the handle and pull the door open. As I step inside, my eyes land on her and my cheeks become wet. My mother's words ring through my mind. *Toughen up, be a man,* she would tell five-year-old me. *Real men don't cry. You're a prince, emotions aren't allowed.* I've been hiding my emotions for so long... I didn't realize I was still capable of tears.

My feet move forward against my will. Everything within me wants to run away and pretend this isn't happening.

When I reach her side, I grab her limp hand, bringing it to my lips. "I promise we will fix this," I murmur into it.

Looking around, I notice that Jack and the panther queen are absent. Grief is the only thing I see on the remaining faces. My mind is racing to find a solution. Who could save our girl?

"A witch. We need a witch!" Spence says from the corner, his voice booming in the hushed space.

"Wait, that could work," Reid agrees from behind me.

"Does anyone know a witch?" I ask, looking around from face to face.

Everyone shakes their heads, including Lia's adoptive parents. My heart sinks; I was hoping they would at least know of someone in the area.

"Witches don't really mingle with shifters. They're a secretive bunch," Lia's adoptive dad says.

"I was hoping it was different off our island," Reid's face drops. "They don't teach us much about them."

I try to recall anything we learned about witches. We've never really had any dealings with them. Mostly, we leave them alone and they don't bother us. I wish I had more information.

"I will go check with the pack alpha," I decide aloud as I take off out of the room.

Running through the compound, I find myself in front of the steel door containing the holding cells. I lift my hand and knock loudly. The bear shifters open the door and peer out.

"I don't know if you want to see what's happening in here cub," one of them says, eyeing me nervously.

"I'm not a cub, and I need to talk to the alpha," I growl back.

He stares at me a moment, indecision flashing across his face before he opens the door further. I squeeze through before he can change his mind and continue on to the holding cells where I find the alpha, panther queen, and Jack. They chained the lion beta flat against the wall inside his cell, while a bear stands in front of him.

Jack sees me out of the corner of his eye and turns to address me. "Kenton, what are you doing here?"

"I have a question for the alpha," I reply, tearing my eyes away from the lion to meet Jack's.

"Spit it out, son," the alpha says, walking in front of me blocking my view of the lion beta.

"Do you know any witches we can contact? Maybe they could help Lia. This whole thing stinks of magic," I ask, standing tall under his weighted gaze.

"Why didn't I think of that?" Jack growls from behind the alpha.

"It is a solid idea," the panther queen agrees.

"I know of a few, but shifters and witches rarely mingle," the alpha says thoughtfully. He turns around addressing the cats behind him. "Do you have this?"

"We do," Queen Adrielle says in a low, menacing voice.

"Follow me, son," Alpha turns around and gestures.

I fall into step beside him, following him through the compound in silence. When we reach what appears to be his office, he ushers me inside and closes the door behind us.

"I have a witch friend, but this information cannot leave this room," he levels a hard stare at me.

"I understand, sir. I wouldn't ask, but I need to save my mate," I explain, pleading with my eyes.

"That's why I'm helping you. I've known Amelia since she was first adopted into this clan. I will always consider her clan," he says.

"I understand. She's a special girl," I reply, letting out a breath I didn't realize I was holding. He will help us.

He grabs his phone and dials a number. It feels like we wait for ages while it rings to see if someone answers. Finally, a woman's voice comes from the other end.

"Hello?" she answers.

"Jenn, you're on speakerphone," the alpha warns her.

"I'm assuming this isn't a social call then," she sighs.

"I wish it was, but no," he replies before explaining what happened.

"So, they gave this panther shifter devil's flower, but the orthosiphon put her in a coma?" she asks, her voice full of shock.

"That's what happened," I growl, before realizing I should stay quiet. Alpha shoots me a dirty look.

"I think the kid is right, this reeks of magic. I'll dig around and see what I can come up with," she replies then hangs up.

"Now all we can do is wait. Grab your cats and go for a run. You are all wound too tight and it will get explosive if you don't," the alpha says, dismissing me from the office.

CHAPTER FIVE

KENTON

I leave the office and make my way back to the medical ward. Alpha is right, the other's need to run, and even though I just returned from one, I know it wouldn't hurt to burn off some of this anxiety.

When I enter Lia's room, I can feel everyone's gaze on me. I clear my throat. "Alpha suggests we go for a run to blow off steam," I tell them, then my eyes land on Rachael. "Sorry you can't join us."

"It's ok," she gives a sad smile, rubbing her belly.

"We'll stay with you," Lia's mom walks over and pats Rachael's hand.

I turn around exiting the room, the others on my heels. When we make it to the front door, we run into Jack.

"Where's the alpha? I forgot to ask him about shifting on his lands," Jack says, his voice flat, but agitation flashes across his face.

"He already told me to go run," I shrug at him, giving him a cocky grin.

He rolls his eyes but joins our little group. We head deep into the woods behind the compound before letting our cats out. We reach a small clearing and strip off our clothes silently then shift.

Once we are all cats, we take off running, chasing each other, just enjoying the freedom our animal half gives us. A brief respite from reality. We continue until we are all panting. We make our way back to the clearing, shift back, and get dressed.

Reality sets back in again and I try my hardest not to let the guilt consume me. I should have curbed my anger and talked to Lia when I had the chance. What if she blames me for my mother's actions? She needs to know I will always pick her over everyone else, including my mother. Worse yet, what if I never get to talk to her again? I really blew it this time. I just hope I get the chance to make it up to her.

We were off running and blowing off steam while our mate is stuck in an endless sleep.

By the time we make it back to the compound, the sun is setting. We spent longer running than I had realized. The alpha is leaning against the building waiting for us as we approach.

"Wasn't sure if you were ever coming back," he grins, but his joke falls flat.

I stare at him trying to figure out how to reply. I don't want to offend him since he's helping us, but his comment rubs me the wrong way, like I would abandon my mate. Why is everyone questioning my loyalty?

"What's your name, anyway? I notice everyone just calls you Alpha," I settle on, trying to change the subject.

"In bear culture, the alpha no longer has a name. But before I became alpha, I was called Adam," he replies. "Since you're not a bear, feel free to use my name."

I nod dumbly. I'm so off my game right now; I don't know how to act. I'm supposed to be seen as strong, capable, almost a robot. I wasn't. How the hell am I going to get through this?

"Anyway, I was waiting on you to get back because I heard back from Jenn. She's on her way here now because according to her whatever she has to say she doesn't want to risk being overheard," he explains, his face growing serious.

"What are you guys talking about?" Spence asks, a confused look on his face.

Fuck! I forgot to fill them in on what I found out. I run over the brief conversation and who Jenn is as we make our way back to Adam's office.

When I finish talking, Dom looks at me. "Hopefully, she has good news," he says, his voice trembling with emotion.

He always seems like a hardass, but I'm convinced he feels everything deeper than anyone else. As we approach the office, Jack excuses himself to go check on Rachael and Lia.

When Adam opens the door, I see it's already occupied. One of his betas is standing uncomfortably next to the desk, as a petite woman with a black pixie cut is propped on the chair behind the desk.

"Good, you're here. I'm out of here," the beta says, glancing nervously at the woman before bolting out the door.

"I guess witches make your bear nervous," she chuckles as she stands up and vacates the alpha's seat.

He shakes his head, the corner of his mouth twitching in his attempt to hide a smile. "What's so secretive you needed to scare my beta," he asks, his eyes still alight with humor.

Her face becomes serious, and she leans forward, speaking low, "I did some poking around. The lion queen commissioned an order for the Nightshade Aether coven to alter a specific toxin. This is some strong magic."

"Who are they?" I ask, knowing next to nothing about witches and their covens.

"They are a coven of dark witches. I wouldn't touch them

with a ten-foot pole. Rumor is they will do anything for a price. This lends credence to it…" Jenn explains patiently.

"Does that mean you can't help us?" Reid asks, his voice strangled.

"Not me personally, no. But I can take you to the only ones who might," she replies. "The Dunbraind Enclave Island coven is her only hope. They have the best witches in the world."

"Would they really help us?" Dom asks, eyeing her warily.

"I believe they would. Considering she's the queen our seers have been prophesying about for centuries," she stares at him with a fierceness that makes her appear to be much larger than she is.

My eyes widen in shock. It never occurred to me that the prophecy came from the witches, but it makes sense. It's exceedingly rare for a royal to have the power of prophecy.

"Where is this coven? Are we gambling taking her there? You said you believe, but you don't know?" I assault her with questions, trying to keep my temper in check.

"Their location is a secret that I'm not permitted to share. My crone took a risk telling me and allowing me to help you. I can't promise they will help, but I believe they will. If you stay here, she will not have a chance. Your call." She shrugs.

"We need to get everything ready to leave as soon as possible," Reid says, his brow bunched in thought.

"I've packed what I need so I'm ready whenever you are," Jenn shrugs.

"I'll try to arrange transport," Adam says, reaching for his phone.

"I'm sure Queen Adrielle's plane is still nearby," Spence suggests.

"You're right. Go find Carter and have him ready Amelia for transport. I'll go talk to the queen," Adam orders as he stands up.

We shuffle out of the room and make our way back to Lia's room. Hopefully, Carter is nearby but when we enter the room, he isn't present. I let the other guys take care of explaining everything to Jack and Rachael, while I explore further down the hallway, trying to find where Carter could be.

The hall ends in a door to an office. I knock and hear Carter mumble to come in. Opening the door, I find him sitting on a sofa, looking haggard.

"Is she worse?" he looks up, fear radiating off of him.

"No, nothing like that. Alpha asked me to have you get Lia ready for transport. We are taking her to a witch coven to see if they can help her," I explain, attempting to be gentle with the poor omega.

He nods as he listens. "I'll see if he wants me to travel with you," he replies nervously as he rises to his feet.

"Get Lia ready, please. I'll go check with the alpha for you," I reply, turning around and walking out.

As soon as I'm in the hallway, I take off in a run to the cells, where Adam said he was going. He's coming out of the steel door as I approach.

"Everything ok?" he asks, his brows pulled together in concern.

"Yeah, Carter wanted to know if you want him to travel with us," I explain.

He tilts his head in thought for a moment. "Go ask Jenn if it's necessary. He will be uncomfortable with so many dominant shifters, but I don't want to put Lia in unnecessary risk," he answers as Queen Adrielle joins him.

"What is it you wanted to speak about?" she asks as I turn and jog back to his office to look for Jenn. I'm feeling like a courier.

When I arrive, I knock on the door as I open it so not to catch her off guard.

"Adam wanted me to ask you if we need to bring the nurse along," I blurt out as soon as I'm through the doorway.

"It would probably be wise. Someone should monitor her condition while we are traveling. The witches will take over once we arrive though," she answers. "I'll follow you back to the girl."

I nod my head and walk this time as we return to the medical ward, so she can keep up. We stay silent, me not knowing what to say to this stranger. When we reach Lia's room, Carter has her on a stretcher, ready to go. His eyes dart up to mine, and I give a small nod to let him know he's coming. He immediately shoots his eyes down to his feet, and I can feel the anxiety rolling off of him. Hopefully, he can make it through this trip without losing it.

Rachael is watching him and stands up, placing a hand gently on his shoulder. "I promise, you are safe with us," she tells him in a soft voice.

He visibly relaxes at her words. I don't know why none of us thought of reassuring him in this way. There aren't very many omegas in the Huntsman Clan, and those we have are kept separate and protected.

"Everyone ready to go?" Adam says from behind me. I didn't hear them approach, letting me know just how stressed out I am.

Lia's adoptive parents move to join us, and the alpha stops them. "I'm afraid you need to stay here," he tells them gently.

Her mom looks like she wants to argue, but her dad lays a hand on her arm and shakes his head slightly.

"Let's get moving," Queen Adrielle commands, and our small party follows her out the door.

CHAPTER SIX

SPENCER

We follow the queen out to a waiting limo with a cargo van behind it. I look back and forth between the vehicles, torn. The van is obviously for Lia and I don't want to be separated from her, but I don't think there is room for all of us and I'm sure the others are thinking the same thing.

"Carter will ride with Amelia. The rest of you get in the limo," Queen Adrielle orders.

I sigh and do as she says, though it's killing me. I usually try to mask my feelings with humor, but I just don't have it in me at the moment. We ride to the airport in silence. No one wants to speak what we are all thinking. Will this work? Can the witches save our girl?

I want to believe they can, no; I need to believe they can. The scenery outside flashes by in a blur as the thoughts build on top of each other in my mind like a house of cards, ready to topple at the slightest wind and send me into a downward spiral of anger and angst.

We arrive at the small municipal airport a short time later

where Queen Adrielle's private jet awaits. We load up and Carter makes sure Lia is secure before we take off.

"Y'all need to quit acting like someone died," Jenn says once we are in the air. "I'm confident the Dunbraind Enclave can save her."

"I'm glad one of us is," Dom mutters, earning a dirty look from Queen Adrielle.

"She's right. Let's be positive," Queen Adrielle says. "I've heard of this clan, in fact many years ago I used to know a witch from the clan. They are the best in the world. Let's put a movie on or something"

Kenton sighs but gets up and has the flight attendant put a movie on. We all watch quietly until they serve dinner. I wonder how far away this island is. No one offered any information, so it could be anywhere.

"Where exactly are we going?" I finally get the nerve to ask.

"It's off the coast of England," Jenn says vaguely. Damn, this will be a long flight. I lay my chair back into bed form and take a catnap. I have had little rest since Lia was taken, and it's catching up to me.

A gentle shaking rouses me a few moments later. "What?" I ask groggily.

"We're getting ready to land," Rachael explains.

I glance at my phone and my jaw drops open. I thought I had just closed my eyes, but I slept for nearly five hours. I set my seat up and put on the seatbelt.

Looking out the window, I don't even see an island for the plane to land on and notice Jenn is absent.

"How are we going to land in the middle of the ocean?" I ask, confused.

"There's a landing strip, right over there," Dom points out the window.

I look in the direction he's pointing, and sure enough there is a tiny airport, but that's all that is on the island.

"Is this some kind of joke?" I question them, looking around.

Reid snickers, and Dom fights to keep a straight face. "Jenn explained the island is cloaked much like our own. We won't be able to see the rest of it until they want us to see it," Queen Adrielle says, smiling. Great, even she's trying not to laugh at me. That's what I get for sleeping.

I plaster on my goofy smile, so they don't know that their ribbing is getting to me. We get our stuff together and follow Jenn off of the plane where a tall, thin woman is waiting at the edge of the runway. Her hair is blowing in the wind, bright red curls that must hit below her butt if it was still.

She steps forward, her mere presence exuding power unlike anything I've felt before. It gives me hope that Jenn is right, and these witches can help our Lia.

"I'm Davina of the Dunbraind Enclave Island coven, state your business on our island," her voice booms over us.

Jenn drops to her knees immediately, the rest of us take the cue and mimic her. "I'm sorry for dropping in unannounced, but you are the only ones who can help this poor panther shifter. The Nightshade Aether coven altered a toxin and poisoned her. She's the one the prophecy speaks of," Jenn explains, keeping her eyes firmly placed on the pavement in front of her.

"Rise sister. Where is this girl?" Davina asks, looking around.

"On the plane with the medic still," Kenton answers, pointing at the plane.

She brushes by us, all still kneeling on the ground, and rushes up on the plane. I look at the others. Dom shrugs back as we get up and follow her.

"What was she given?" Davina asks as soon as I enter the plane.

"Devil's flower. We gave her orthosiphon to counteract it, but since they altered it, it put her in a coma," Carter explains, his eyes on the ground and body visibly shaking.

"Calm yourself shifter, I mean you no harm. We will have to take her to the village for the coven to help. This won't be a simple fix," she explains, speaking gently to the scared bear.

"But you think you can help her?" I ask, my voice full of hope.

"If anyone can, it will be us, but I'm not making any promises," she meets my eyes, a determination burning behind hers.

Carter readies Lia for unloading and I glance out the window while we wait. My jaw drops as I watch the ocean recede and the island melt into view. We are on the edge of what appears to be a large city.

"Nifty isn't it?" Davina asks from behind me.

"It really is. I swore that was the ocean..." my voice trails off.

We finally get Lia off the plane and into a van that appears on the side of the runway. I question how we will all fit, but Jenn shakes her head and pushes me forward towards the door. Once I enter, my jaw drops again. The van appears to be a normal size on the outside, but on the inside it's huge, the size of a large school bus.

"How?" Jack asks.

"Magic," Davina laughs. "It's bigger on the inside."

"Wow," Jack replies, looking around, his eyes wide.

Once we are all loaded into the van, it takes off, though there isn't anyone driving it.

"All of our vehicles run off of magic and are self-driving. Better for the environment," Davina explains.

We drive through the busy city. Everything is clean and

modern. Everything appears to run on magic or solar energy. Who knows, it might be a mixture of both.

"The heads of the coven are downtown," Davina explains as we move through the city.

Occasionally, she points out different landmarks around the city and gives us an explanation about them. It was founded by the coven when they split apart from one on the mainland, nearly one hundred years ago. One of their goals is to make as small of an impact on the environment as possible, so they've merged magic and technology to run everything.

"This river supplies the water to the entire community," she says as we pass over a bridge. "We use magic to treat the water, so no chemicals are involved."

"Have you always lived here?" Jenn asks, her eyes bright with wonder.

"I have. I was born here, but have traveled around the world," Davina explains. "Nothing compares to home."

"I wish my home was like this," Jenn replies, a hint of sadness in her voice.

Davina gives her a strange look, but it passes across her face quickly. Shortly after crossing the bridge, we arrive at a tall glass building. The van pulls to a stop in front of the double doors with chrome handles. Davina jumps out, telling us to wait here before running into the building.

*S*itting in the van is incredibly difficult. I want to get out and explore. Dissect exactly how everything is working, but most of all get Lia help. It's killing me she's like this, and it's partially our fault. If she hadn't gone out alone, maybe she would have never been taken.

I've worked hard to keep my guilty thoughts to myself. I made Wood promise me he wouldn't share them. Though he wasn't happy about it. He doesn't think we should feel this way. Sometimes, I think it would be easier to be a cat all the time.

Before long, Davina returns to the van, followed by twelve other witches. They quickly unload Lia and take her in the building, before any of us can move. The van door slams shut, and Dom rushes it, pushing against it but it won't open. He throws his full body weight against it, but nothing budges.

Just as he is about to slam into it a second time, Davina opens the door from the outside and he falls out, growling at her as he does.

"I'm so sorry. I forgot the van had locks to keep nonmagical passengers contained," she gives us a sheepish smile. "Please follow me."

She turns around and waits by the doors to the building. As soon as we are all out of the van, she opens the door and ushers us inside, taking the lead.

"The thirteen strongest witches run the coven. This is headquarters, so if anyone can help your friend, it will be here," she explains as she leads us through the foyer and down a hallway.

"I only saw twelve witches come out with you," Jenn points out.

"Because I'm number thirteen, silly," Davina laughs, her voice sounding like tinkling bells.

We reach the end of the hallway, and Davina stops dead in her tracks. "Wait here. They are working a spell and we shouldn't interrupt."

I stop, but everything in me wants to rush forward to my mate. I hate being separated from her, even for a short time. What if she doesn't make it?

"Stop thinking like that," Wood growls at me.

"I can't help it," I tell my panther.

"It still isn't your fault. We were at her childhood home. It was supposed to be safe," Wood reminds me.

Logically, I know he's right. But that doesn't mean I can get my emotions on the same page. We stand in the hallway, just waiting around for Davina to let us go forward.

She tilts her head sideways then motions for us to continue, staying quiet as she does so. She opens the door to a large room. Lia lies on a table with the twelve witches surrounding her.

"It's as you said. They magically altered the toxin to interact with the cure," a silver-haired woman walks towards us. "We will have to alter the orthosiphon to cure the new toxin."

"Yes, Mother," Davina nods her head and takes off without another word.

"I'm Myrna, the crone," the silver-haired woman introduces herself.

"Davina is retrieving orthosiphon, and we will alter its makeup to save your friend. She has a particularly important destiny," Myrna explains to us.

"Thank you for taking the time to treat my granddaughter," Adrielle steps forward, bowing to the crone.

"My pleasure, panther," she smiles gently at the queen.

"It's been too long," Adrielle smiles back at the old woman before they embrace.

Interesting. Maybe her friend is more important than she let on.

The two older women move off to the corner chatting quietly with their heads together like old friends. I'm curious, but not enough to ask the queen her personal business.

Dom feels different as he walks up to the two older women.

"Excuse me, Queen Adrielle; if you already know these witches, why didn't you suggest bringing Lia here yourself?" he asks through clenched teeth.

"Oh," the queen replies, a look of shock on her face. "Myrna and I haven't seen or spoken in many years. I had no way of contacting her and this island is a very well-kept secret."

"Sorry," he mutters as he walks back to join us.

The queen gives him a strange look before going back to her conversation.

Davina returns with a large supply of orthosiphon and the witches quickly get to work, dividing it into smaller portions.

"This may take a while. We have guest rooms on the third floor. Why don't you all go freshen up and rest? We will send

Davina back to you once we've made any progress," Myrna says.

I open my mouth to protest, but Queen Adrielle shakes her head at me and I quickly shut it. Davina leads us away from Lia, to the foyer where the elevators are. We ride in silence then make our way into each room as she opens them.

The guys and I are sharing one room, which isn't a problem except our nerves are all frayed. As soon as we enter the room, Dom paces the length of it. The rest of us find a corner and sit. The weight of everything that's happened seems to settle in my chest while the surrounding electricity seems to intensify. We are all at our breaking points, waiting and wondering what will happen next.

"I can't believe they made us leave her," Dom growls as he paces back and forth.

"At least they are helping her," I remind him.

"Who knows what they're really doing! They could be killing her and leaving us up here to suffer," he screams in my face.

"Do you really believe that? I don't think the queen would have left her granddaughter with them if she didn't trust them," I try to point out.

"You're too trusting, all of you are," Dom growls then stomps into the bathroom, slamming the door behind him.

He might be right, we all have trusted the very person who caused this to happen, him included, but I didn't feel any ill intent from these witches who are trying to help our girl.

There's a TV and sitting area on the far side of the room. Kenton walks over to the burgundy sofa and plops down before turning on the television.

"Might as well try to keep our minds occupied while we wait," he shrugs.

The rest of us join him while Dom continues to sulk in the bathroom alone. We've learned to leave him to his moods. If we try to talk to him any further, he will never calm down.

"Be honest, Kenton; this strong act isn't cutting it. Remember, we can feel you," I say, getting his attention. "How are you really doing?"

He's silent for a moment, then the damn breaks. Tears pour down his cheeks. My heart breaks for my brother and I'm not sure how to react. Spence wraps an arm around his shoulder while Kenton puts his hands to his face and sobs.

"I didn't talk to her when she asked me too. I was too mad. She will hate me. My fucking mother did this. What if she blames me too?" he unloads. "What if she never wakes up? I fucked up so bad this time."

"Why didn't you talk to us sooner?" Vance asks. "She won't hate you. She's our mate. We all mess up, you just have to apologize after the witches wake her up, and they will wake her up."

"How can you be so sure? What if she pushes me out?" Kenton meets his eyes. "What if she breaks us all up?"

"Lia isn't like that. Remember, she didn't want to date any of us because she was afraid of breaking up our group. You're here with her and not with your mother, that counts for a lot," Vance reassures him. "The witches have to fix her; I can't believe anything else."

"Let's try to watch a movie, yeah?" Spence says after a moment of silence.

"That's a good idea," Kenton replies, regaining control of his emotions. He grabs the remote and puts one on and we settle back and watch in silence.

I try to focus on the movie, but my mind keeps drifting back to Lia. I hate this waiting and not knowing. It's the worst torture I can think of.

A while later, Spence is shaking my shoulder. I somehow drifted off. "Davina is at the door," he mumbles.

I sit up, immediately alert. Did they find something? Is she awake now?

I rush to follow him to the hallway where the rest of our group is waiting and we follow Davina silently back to the room where they have Lia. I open my mouth to ask but Jack shakes his head no at me, and I glare at him.

"What's going on?" I ask, lifting my chin in defiance.

"We need your help, hurry along," Davina replies.

We follow her back to the room they are keeping Lia in. When we enter, Lia is lying on the table, unchanged and my heart sinks. I was hoping her showing up meant that they figured out how to help her.

The crone steps forward. "Thank you for your patience. I know it's hard to see a loved one in this condition. We believe we've found the cure, but we need the blood of her mates to do the spell," she explains.

Dom steps forward offering his wrist. "Take it," he says through gritted teeth, staring the old woman down.

"I agree, anything for Lia," I join him.

The rest of the guys do the same and a smile forms on the old crone's face.

"She's very lucky to have so many people who love her. She'll need you in the storm to come."

CHAPTER EIGHT

I've stayed quiet since we got Lia back, but no one seemed to notice. Sometimes I feel like I'm invisible, but it can be a good thing. I need time to process what's happening. Only Dom and Jack understand the pain of losing family permanently, and it's making me flash back to my mom.

She had cancer for so long, but no one could help her. With all the witches' magic, some things just can't be cured, or at least that's what our healers said. I'm scared the same is happening with our mate. I don't even know if blood magic will work, and I can't afford to get my hopes up.

The witches line up in front of us with their ceremonial knives. Davina escorts the queen, Jack, and Rachael out of the room while the crone runs through the ceremony with the five of us.

"We will use our athames to cut your arm then collect a small amount of blood from each of you in this chalice," she begins.

"Why in a chalice? Does she have to drink our blood?" Reid asks, his expression filled with horror.

"No child, it's just a part of our ceremonial tools," she smiles sweetly at him. "After we have your blood, we will perform the spell over the orthosiphon then make it into a serum that can be injected. Then if everything works out correctly, she will wake up."

"What if it doesn't work the way you think?" Dom asks, his eyes hard.

"Then, we will have to think of something else, but I'm confident this will work," the crone meets his eyes with power shining through her own.

"Just do it," my voice comes out small, almost pleading.

She nods once and the witches approach us, grabbing our arms and cutting at the same time. I hold back a hiss as the knife slices through the skin on my forearm. It burns with magic. As the blood is being collected, they chant; the power building in the room makes it hard to breathe.

I watch as they pour the blood over the long stem of little white flowers with long white whiskers growing out of them, and it morphs into a clear liquid as their magic swirls around it, splashing into the bowl. My eyes widen in awe at the sight. These have to be the most powerful witches in existence to so easily turn a plant into a liquid.

The crone steps forward and sucks up the liquid in a syringe. I hold my breath as she approaches Lia and injects it into the IV still placed in her arm. We watch with bated breath, waiting for something to happen.

"Is it working?" Kenton asks anxiously.

"Give it a minute," Davina tells him.

We stare on and her eyes flutter. It worked! She's waking up. Her eyes open all the way and she looks around, panic marring her beautiful face. I rush forward and grab her hand. The others on my heels.

"It's ok, Princess. They saved you," I whisper, tears streaming down my face.

The relief I feel is astronomical. I don't think I really believed they could wake her up. As she looks around, her face is full of confusion; otherwise, she seems comfortable.

"Who are you?" she asks, giving me a puzzled look. "For that matter, who am I?"

"What the hell? Why can't she remember us?" Dom growls as he paces back and forth. "Why can't I feel her yet?"

"I'm not sure. We will have to run more tests," the crone says, rushing forward with a look of concern on her face.

My heart breaks all over again. She's awake, but she has no memory. How is this possible?

"It's weird. I feel like you five belong to me, and a voice in my head says you're my mates, but I don't recognize you," Lia says, her voice tinged with sorrow.

"It's ok, Trouble. We will figure out how to help you remember," Kenton says.

"Kylah says your name is Kenton?" she responds.

"That's right. And this is Vance, that's Spence, Reid is over there, and Dom is pacing," he explains gently.

"Kylah says to trust you. I'm not sure why, but I feel like she isn't just a strange voice in my head," she says, looking around for confirmation.

"She's your panther. You're a black panther shifter," Reid reminds her.

"Oh wow. I have a lot to learn," her eyes grow large.

"Rest for now. We will work on your memory later," the crone tells her, shooing us away.

Davina leads us out in the hallway to where the queen, Jack, and Rachael are waiting. I explain to them what happened and watch as their faces fall. I hope this is a temporary side effect. I couldn't imagine going through life not knowing my past, even the painful parts.

We make our way back up to our rooms to rest and hopefully sleep for a few hours. Since the crone separated us from our mate, I don't know how much sleep any of us will get, but we all need it. We've been running on nearly empty for days.

Once we are in the room, we quietly get ready for bed and sprawl out, two to a bed and Dom takes the couch. I close my eyes and try to fall asleep, but thoughts keep running through my head. What if she never regains her memory? Is she going to always be apart from us? Will our bond ever return? I slowly drift off as these questions keep replaying through my mind.

I wake up the next morning with a foot in my face. I push it off to see Reid sleeping with his head at the foot of our bed.

"Wake up you lug," I kick him.

He groans as he attempts to reach for the nightstand where he left his glasses. Instead, since he's now backwards in the bed, he loses his balance and falls to the floor.

"What the hell?" he asks confused.

"You turned around in your sleep. Must have been some dream." I laugh loudly, waking the others.

"I'm starving. When's the last time we ate?" Kenton asks.

"Too long ago," I reply. "Let's go find food, surely they have some somewhere."

We get up and dress for the day then leave the room. Kenton leads us down to the lobby. Hopefully, we will run into someone who can point us to a kitchen or restaurant. When we reach the ground floor, there's no one in sight. The building appears to be sleeping. The elevator behind us dings and the rest of our group joins us.

"Did you get any rest?" I ask them.

"I slept like a rock," Rachael says, holding onto Jack's arm. His jaw is ticking, and his eyes are bloodshot. Apparently, he couldn't rest at all.

"Davina called, she's meeting us here to get breakfast," Queen Adrielle informs us.

"Finally! I'm dying of starvation here," Spence says dramatically, clutching his chest.

The queen shakes her head at him but grants his theatrics a small smile. The van that brought us here pulls up outside the glass front and we rush out to join the witch who promised us food.

"Where is Carter and Jenn?" Kenton asks when we reach Davina.

Crap, I didn't even notice they were missing. When was the last time I saw either of them?

"We put them up in a hotel down the street. They didn't really need to be here," she shrugs.

We load up in the van and it takes us a few blocks away to a small diner.

"This is one of my favorite places to eat," Davina says with a smile as we unload from the van and make our way inside.

It somewhat reminds me of our mom and pop diner back home with the vibe of it. Small tables in the center with booths lining the walls. The waitress pushes tables together to accommodate our larger party and we settle in to look at the menu.

When she returns, we place our orders, her eyes growing wide at the amount of food each of us request.

"Any news on Lia's memory?" Reid asks.

"I'm afraid not yet, but I'm sure they will figure it out," Davina shoots him a reassuring smile.

We chat for a while until the waitress returns with our food floating behind her, trailing her like a magical puppy dog.

I dig in and groan when I taste the first bite. Whatever magic these witches used to make their food makes it taste wonderful. Not a word is spoken while we shovel food into our mouths. Too many meals have been skipped lately, and that doesn't go over well with growing shifters.

Davina's phone rings and she excuses herself to take the call. By the time she returns, we've finished eating. The queen pays for our bill and we follow Davina back out to the van.

"Great news! The crone thinks she's found the reason for the memory loss," Davina exclaims.

CHAPTER NINE

LIA

Wake up in the same strange room as yesterday. My head is still foggy and I can't recall anything from my past. It's getting really frustrating already. At least I have Kylah, and she seems to have kept most of our memories.

The look on that poor boy's face yesterday when I asked who he was, haunted my dreams. I can still feel his heart breaking. Hopefully, these witches know what they are doing and can fix my broken mind.

"If they can't fix you, I'll keep reminding you," Kylah stretches in the back of my mind.

"I want to know myself though," I sigh inside.

I really need to go to the bathroom, but they've left me alone in here. I stand up, wobbling for a second before I catch my balance. Making my way slowly to the door, I find it locked and panic.

"Let me out of here!" I scream at the top of my lungs while banging on the door.

The door opens and the old woman from last night rushes in.

"I'm so sorry dear. We didn't think you'd wake up so soon," she apologizes in a soothing voice.

"I need to pee," I tell her, doing a little dance trying to hold it.

"Follow me, the bathroom is this way," she gives me a sympathetic smile.

I follow her and have never been so glad to see a toilet in my life. I attempt to wash up in the sink after with moderate success. The next thing I need is a shower and clean clothes, but I somehow don't think it's anyone else's priority right now.

Another witch is waiting for me outside of the restroom and leads me back to the room I woke up in. The rest of the witches are all present now and the group of guys from last night.

They all look like they want to approach me but are forcing themselves to hang back. I give a small wave before sitting in the closest chair I can find. I hate feeling this drained.

"I can almost feel them again," Kylah cries out.

I feel her distress at what she calls her missing bonds, but I don't remember them, so there's nothing for me to miss. The old woman steps forward, and a hush falls over the room.

"We think we've found a spell to return the girl's memories. It appears the magic attempted to severe her bonds but was unsuccessful. Instead, it just masked them, her missing memories are a side effect of that," she explains, talking more to the group of people I'm supposed to know.

"Fix her then," the one Kylah calls Dom growls.

The crone nods to him and the witches surround me. One places stones around my feet, while another places a bundle of leaves on my lap. Anxiety of the unknown builds in my chest.

They form a circle and begin chanting. The leaves in my lap aren't on fire, but they produce smoke. As I breathe it in, I feel light-headed. The room begins to spin, faster and faster, until it all fades to black.

My eyes pop open a short while later. I remember who I am! I look around and see my mates, brother Jack, sister Rachael, and my grandmother staring at me anxiously.

"I remember you," I croak out weakly, before falling back into the darkness.

When my eyes next open, I'm laid in a soft bed with a soft green comforter pulled up to my chin. I look over and Rachael is sitting in a chair next to the bed. My bonds snap back into place. I can feel the anxiety rolling off my mates in waves.

"Look who's returned to the land of the living," she smiles at me.

"Where is everyone? Are they ok? " I ask, worried about my mates. "Where are we? How did we get here? What is going on?"

"We are on an island of the witches who saved you, everyone is fine. First, why don't you take a shower and I'll get you something to eat," she prompts me.

"Do I have any clean clothes?" I ask.

"I've got you covered. I grabbed your bag before we left. I didn't think any of the guys would have thought about it," she chuckles, pointing to my suitcase parked at the end of the bed.

"You're the best sister ever! I'd hug you, but no one should be subjected to that," I wrinkle my nose, thinking about how bad I must smell.

"Go get cleaned up. I'll ask Davina to bring you some food," Rachael shakes her head, shooing me into the bathroom.

I shower as fast as I can, but it still takes much too long to get my hair clean. By the time I'm dressed, there's food waiting for me. I wonder who Davina is, but quickly become consumed with getting food in my mouth as fast as possible.

"You ready to see your guys now?" Rachael asks.

"Yes!" I exclaim around a mouthful of food, not caring about how gross it probably is.

No sooner than I respond, they come through the door. Dom rushing forward first, scooping me up in his arms, separating me from my food.

I'm passed around between one set of strong arms to the next, though no one seems to want to let me go.

"Can I finish eating? Then you can hold me however long you want to," I offer, my stomach still growling.

"I thought we lost you forever, Kitten. I couldn't feel anything at all," Dom says, his voice hoarse with emotion.

"I can feel you again," I whisper. "I won't go anywhere alone again. I'm sorry."

"Don't you apologize. It's not your fault. We all thought it was safe in your hometown," Reid chimes in, his eyes haunted.

"It's not your fault either," I point out. I can feel that he's blaming himself. "What all happened after they took me? I remember nothing."

"You don't remember being kidnapped? Or anything?" Dom asks giving me a strange look.

"The last thing I remember is being at my parents' house. Then I wake up here," I explain.

I didn't realize how empty I felt until they were back. I dig back into my food while they catch me up on everything they've learned since I was first taken.

My jaw drops open when they explain Kenton's mom was behind the entire thing. I would have never imagined one of the queens would do this. That Kenton's mom would betray her own son.

"What are we going to do?" I ask, ready to fight. "She needs to pay."

"Hold your horses, Killer. We can't take on a queen on our own," Spence points out.

"Good thing we have one on our side," Kenton replies, his voice emotionless.

I wonder how this is affecting him. To be betrayed by the one person who is supposed to keep you safe, to love you. How is this going to affect us? Is he going to blame me for his mother's actions? Will he still want to be with me? We really need to talk.

"Make that two," Jack says from the doorway. I didn't even hear him come in.

"What do you mean two?" I ask, a bit confused. I know one must be my grandmother.

"I called my mom and let her know what's going on. She already sees you like a daughter, so she's on the phone with Queen Adrielle right now plotting what to do," Rachael grins, looking wicked.

"So all we can do is wait?" I groan.

"Afraid so, Jet," Reid shoot a sympathetic smile.

"Are we at least allowed to explore?" I ask walking over to the window.

I feel cooped up and Kylah wants to run. I doubt the witches want a shifter running around their territory, but maybe if I can get outside it will be enough.

"I don't know? Maybe Davina can take us around. We should see if we can check in with Carter and Jenn at least, to let them know Lia is better," Vance suggests.

"I'll call her. She gave me her number," Rachael says, pulling out her phone.

We wait and listen to Rachael's side of the conversation.

She smiles as she hangs up the phone. "Let's go downstairs. We will go visit Carter and Jenn for sure, but she said she'd check with the others to see if we can explore," Rachael explains.

I follow with Reid holding one hand and Dom the other as we make our way to the lobby. My eyes open wide when we get off the elevator. The entire front of the building is made of glass. The younger woman with long curly red hair is standing by the doors waiting.

"Hi, I'm Davina," she walks up and introduces herself to me.

"Lia," I smile at her. "Thanks for saving me."

"My pleasure, but I didn't do much. It was the rest of the council that did the heavy lifting. They agreed to let me show you around town as long as you don't get into any trouble. That doable?" She arches an eyebrow and smiles.

"I'd rather not have any more trouble for at least a couple of days." I grin back at her.

We load up in a van that drives itself and head down the road, pulling into the parking lot of a hotel. We unload and follow Davina inside. She turns down a hallway and knocks on doors on either side of the hallway.

Carter, the bear shifter who took care of me opens one and smiles when he sees me. "I wasn't sure when I'd get to see those pretty eyes again," he says, looking down when Kenton growls at him.

"Settle down. He's just being friendly," I chastise him for scaring the poor omega.

"Sorry," my territorial lion shifter grunts back.

The woman who comes out of the other door introduces herself. "I'm Jenn, you must be Lia," she smiles at me.

"Nice to meet you," I reply.

We filter into Jenn's room and the guys recount what all has happened since they separated. Jenn's eyes fill with awe as they recount the spells, Davina chiming in to answer questions when needed.

Once we've finished, we load back up in the van, Jenn joining us but Carter opting to stay at the hotel alone. Davina takes us on a tour of the town. We stop at a park and get out to walk around. It feels good to be outside, stretching my muscles, but Kylah is growing restless.

"Is there anywhere I can shift and run?" I ask Davina.

"It wouldn't be advised here," she says, looking at me thoughtfully. "Let me make a quick call."

She walks a bit further down the path, and we chat among ourselves to give her privacy. After a few minutes, she returns, smiling brightly.

"My friend lives outside of the city and has agreed to let you shift on her land," she says excitedly. "Do you mind if I watch? I've never seen a shifter shift."

"I don't mind if they don't." I shrug, glancing around.

"I can keep you company," Rachael tells Davina.

"You will not shift with them?" She gives her a confused look.

"I won't be able to shift again until the baby is born," Rachael explains, rubbing her belly.

"Fascinating," Davina stares at her belly, eyes wide. "I never thought pregnancy would prevent shifting. What happens if you get pregnant in animal form?"

I bust out laughing then wonder what would happen. Is it a thing?

"Wait, is that a thing?" I ask aloud.

Rachael gives me a small smile and shakes her head. "As far as I know, you can't get pregnant as a cat, but I'll ask my mom to make sure."

"That would be crazy to get stuck in cat form for nine months, or would the gestation cycle change to that of a panther?" I think out loud.

"Um, can we change the subject," Dom asks, shifting back and forth between his feet, looking uncomfortable.

"Sure thing," I wrap my arms around his waist.

We make our way back to the van and drive out of town a ways before stopping in front of a clapboard house.

CHAPTER TEN

We file out of the van, meeting with a young blonde woman.

"Kathryn, thank you for letting us use your land," Davina rushes up and hugs the woman.

"Yes, thank you so much," I add, trying to be polite.

"Head behind the house; just don't kill any of my livestock," she points a finger at us.

"We won't ma'am," Vance replies, nodding his head.

We make our way back behind the house to the tree line and start taking our clothes off. Davina flushes and turns her back to us. "Oh, um, I didn't realize it involved nudity," she stammers.

"If you want to see us shift, you'll have to look," I giggle. "If we tried to shift with our clothes on, we would have to ride back naked."

She turns back around, eyes cast to the ground. "That makes sense. I don't know why I didn't realize that."

I smile at her before turning back to face the open woods. I close my eyes letting Kylah take over, shifting seamlessly before I take off running, not allowing anyone else time to catch up.

"Amazing," I hear Davina say breathlessly behind me.

We run, darting around the trees, until I see Jack come up on my left. I slow down and look back. The others are a good way behind us. I convince Kylah to let us stop for a moment and let them catch up. Feeling playful, I bat at Reid, who is the first to reach us. He lowers his head, wiggles his butt, then pounces, knocking me off my paws. We roll around before I give chase. It's amazing to feel the wind against my face, hear the scattering of smaller creatures looking for safe haven, feel the hard ground, smell the fresh bout of rain that will soon make its way over the island. I soak it all in, allowing everything around me to batter my senses. Because the hard reality of it is, I could very well have fallen victim and none of this would be happening right now.

It's fun to just be free and not worry about human things for a while. We exit in a clearing and I lay down, enjoying the sun on my fur, panting to catch my breath.

"We should head back. Not everyone can shift as long as you," Kylah reminds me.

I huff at her but get to my feet and start back down the path we came from. Halfway there, Reid and I run into the others. They turn around and we amble back to the edge of the woods and shift back.

"I didn't think you were ever coming back," Rachael teases, once we're dressed.

"I could have run longer," I shrug. "... but Kylah was worried about our mates. Can we get something to eat? I'm famished."

"Shifters really do eat a lot," Davina says, her eyes wide.

"You have no idea," I laugh.

We make our way back to the van. The drive back into town seems to go faster, probably because I don't feel so restless now that Kylah got to run. We stop at a restaurant where my grandma meets me with the crone.

"After we eat, we'll return home. A guard will meet us at the airport and be with you at all times, Lia," she says, staring at me.

"Is there any way I can see my parents before we go home? I don't know if they even know I'm okay," I look down, realizing I don't even have my cell phone with me. Now I'm feeling even worse, this is the first time I thought of them.

It must have shown on my face because my grandmother wraps her arms around me. "I called them as soon as you were better and let them know. I'm sorry Christmas didn't go as planned. When this is all over, we will find a way for you all to spend some time together," she promises.

"Thank you," I choke out, a tear running down my cheek. I don't know why I'm suddenly feeling so emotional, but that small gesture really touches me.

"What are we going to do about the Radicals and the other queen?" I ask, glancing at Kenton when I mention his mom. A muscle ticks in his jaw, but that's the only sign that my words affected him.

"I have a plan, but we aren't discussing it here. Let's go eat," she says, swatting my butt lightly.

We go into the restaurant and settle in at a table, order our food, and chow down as soon as it arrives. Once we are all full, we go back to the van and ride to a small landing strip. I give Davina a hug as we're getting ready to board the plane.

"Thank you for saving me," I say, smiling at the witch.

"My pleasure. I gave Rachael my number, so you better keep in touch," she grins back at me.

We load up on the plane, and Kenton sits next to me.

"Lia, I'm sorry I didn't talk to you when you ask me to," he says grabbing my hand. "I'll never put you off again."

"Thank you, but I honestly don't remember," I reply squeezing his hand. "Are we ok? With everything going on…"

"You're my mate. I was worried you wouldn't want me, considering…" he admits.

"I don't blame you for your mother's actions. You're mine to love and protect as much as I am yours," I reply earning a small smile.

CHAPTER ELEVEN

A soft shaking raises me from my sleep. "We're near your hometown sweetie. Wake up," Vance says next to my ear.

"What?" I ask groggily.

"We have to drop Carter and Jenn off so the queen requested your parents be the ones to pick them up. Hurry up so you can see them," he explains.

I look over at my grandma. "Thank you," I say then rush off the plane.

Running down the stairs, I throw myself in my mom's arms. I'm so glad they let me see them for a minute, even though our holiday didn't happen.

"Be safe Amelia. I'm so glad you're all right," my mom says into my hair as she hugs me.

She lets go and my dad pulls me into a bear hug. "You'll do great things. Remember, we always love you."

"Thank you both. I'm sorry we can't stay," I say, looking over my shoulder at the plane. I know everyone wants to get back to take care of matters at the castle.

"Here, open it on the plane," my mom hands me a bag full

of presents. "There are some in there for your new family."

"Thank you, Mom. I love you," I hug her again.

"I love you too," she replies, wiping a tear from her cheek.

I re-board the plane, feeling a mixture of relief and sadness. As soon as we are in the air, I pass out the presents and we open them. Rachael received baby clothes, Jack a watch with a leopard on it, Kenton and the guys all got gift cards.

I wait to open mine last. It's a new cell phone with a letter.

Amelia,

I know your phone was taken when you were kidnapped and it wasn't recovered. We want you to be able to call if you ever need us, so we decided it was the best thing to give you now. The rest of your presents will be waiting for you when you can visit again.

Love,

Mom and Dad

They really are great parents. I wasn't even thinking about presents, but they wanted to make sure I had something.

"Merry Christmas," my grandma says from behind me.

"Is it actually Christmas Day?" I ask, realizing I've lost track of time with everything going on.

"It is. We'll celebrate properly back at the castle. Since you slept earlier, let me explain the plan," she replies, sitting next to me.

I turn my body towards her, giving her my full attention.

"We will act like everything is fine and we suspect nothing. Since it's widely known the Radicals attacked you, the extra guard is easy to explain. Queen Calyope and I are working in the background to provide enough evidence to cement Queen Rani's treason. Just don't talk about any of it. The walls seem to have ears," she explains.

"It will be hard to see her and pretend to be fine," I admit, but I'll do my best. "Do you think she's been behind the Radicals this entire time? Did she kill my mother?"

"Those are some loaded questions, child. I think she's responsible for a lot of what has happened with the panther princesses. I can't prove she was after your mother though," she replies.

"What was my mother like?" I ask.

"You're a lot like her. Always asking questions, stubborn, and throwing herself headfirst at whatever came her way," my grandmother replies, a faraway look in her eyes. "Christmas was her favorite time of year. She always helped the staff decorate the castle, said it needed her personal touch."

"I wish I would have been able to meet her," I reply.

"I know she loved you. She only left you to keep you safe," my grandmother says firmly. "She would be proud of the woman you are becoming."

We settle in and watch a movie, while we fly across the country. The stewardess brings out food, and I finish two full meals. I'm finally starting to feel like myself again.

When we finally land on the island, I didn't expect to feel like I was home, but I do. We ride in silence to the castle. After everything that's happened, it's a bit nerve-wracking to come home to what's waiting for us.

When we pull up out front, a large, muscled man opens the door. "Amelia, meet your new guard AJ. I'd like to see someone get through him," my grandmother gives a satisfied smile.

"Nice to meet you," I say, holding out my hand.

He looks at me opening his arms as if he would hug me than drops them. He glances down at my hand and back up at my face again before taking my hand and shaking it quickly, holding on longer than is comfortable. "You'll be safe with me," he says in a gruff voice.

"Thank you," I reply, offering him an uncomfortable smile. The scowl on his face doesn't change. Something about this man seems familiar, but not. I shake it off and chalk it up to everything that's happened recently.

My grandmother already informed us our rooms are ready in her wing, so we make our way there. It's strange to travel for so long, but it is still daylight when we arrive, although it's evening and I think we lost a day somewhere along the way.

I find appropriate dresses already stocked in the closet and grab the first one my hand lands on. I quickly change into it, brush on makeup, throwing my hair in a messy bun, and call it good. Although we just arrived, it's Christmas, and the clan has a traditional dinner every year. I don't think I'm ready for this. I'm not sure what everyone outside of the royal families knows or doesn't know, and I'm still not a hundred percent sure that I can sit in the same room as Queen Rani and not want to place my hands around her delicate throat and squeeze until I see the light fade from her cold eyes.

The others are waiting in the hallway for us. I guess we cut it really close to the wire due to my brief visit with my parents. It makes me love my grandma that much more for giving me that short but wonderful gift.

AJ stays glued to my left side, a little behind me as we make our way to the main dining room. I can tell it bothers my guys, but they know better than to say anything. AJ is a little too close, stares for a little too long, and acts a little too familiar. It's nothing super out of place, just little things really that seem odd.

We reach the dining room and take our places. Rachael and Jack join the leopard queen and the rest of us stay with my grandmother. I notice Queen Rani staring at us, and I smile and give her a small wave. If not, I would scowl the way Kenton is right now.

AJ stands stoically behind my chair. I notice Rachael now has a guard placed behind her, and the queens, including my grandmother, have menacing guards behind them.

The doors open, and the rest of the clan filter in, filling up the tables. The noise is almost deafening with all the happy chatter happening. It's nice to see people enjoying their holiday, oblivious to the drama going on behind the scenes in the castle.

Once everyone is seated, Queen Calyope stands up, raising her hands above her head to silence the crowd. A hush quickly descends on the dining room as all eyes turn to her.

"Merry Christmas Huntsman Clan. It's with great joy that I can announce our panther princess, Amelia, has been returned to us safe and sound. I would like to propose a toast. To family and clan, may they all have a safe and prosperous holiday," she booms over the crowd, holding up her glass.

The crowd echoes back their cheer, raising their glasses in return. I pick up mine to sip, but AJ slips it from my hand, smelling then tasting it before allowing me to take a drink.

I look over and notice Queen Rani openly glowering at me. I elbow Kenton, who is sitting next to me.

He leans over and whispers, "She's angry that I directly defied her order to come home, but she can't do anything about it. It's on record you are my mate and that bond takes precedence."

"So she's mad because she can't control you," I whisper back just loud enough for him to hear.

He nods yes as my grandmother stands. "We will forgo formal speeches this year. Everyone, please eat and enjoy yourselves," she declares, sitting back down.

The queen's guards, as well as Rachael's, and my all test our food before allowing us to eat.

"Why don't the guys have food testers?" I ask my grandmother.

"They aren't considered royalty, except Kenton and he refused when your other mates weren't given one," she explains.

"If they are my mates, why aren't they royal?" I ask.

"They will be when you are officially married, not until then," she says ending the conversation.

We eat without talking. I spend the time watching all the noble and common class interact. It reminds me of the bear clan, if you take out the royals. I wish I was on the other side, down there with everyone else. I wonder how Dom, Reid, Spence, and Vance feel being thrust up here just because they are my mates. If they feel anything like I do, it's got to be surreal for them. My life has changed so much in such a short period of time… I'm glad they are on the rollercoaster ride with me.

Finally, the dinner ends and the last of the noble and common class filter out so we can leave. AJ glues himself to my side, leading us down back halls I haven't seen before. I wonder if he picked up on something at the dinner I missed. When we get back to our hallway, he ushers us all into my room, placing a finger over his lips telling us to be quiet.

Rachael, Jack, and her guard join us. The guards go over my room with a fine-tooth comb, looking for something. When they are satisfied, AJ tells us to sit. I feel like I'm at school, and the headmaster is talking to us again.

"My guys found something out," he taps on his ear, showing the tiny earpiece hidden there. "The lion queen is planning an attack on Kenton tonight. You will all have guards for the rest of this… altercation."

"How are we going to keep Kenton safe?" I ask, anxiety

and anger warring for control.

"You will all be staying in here tonight. There will be guards in your bedrooms, pretending to be you," the other guard speaks up.

"What if one of them gets hurt then?" I ask, not wanting to see anyone injured.

AJ busts out laughing. "We are the best of the best for a reason, princess. The thugs that Queen Rani uses couldn't make it through our training program. I've always thought it suspicious she wanted her guards so separated."

"Jack and Rachael are moving into the leopard queen's suites until things have settled. She won't risk her grandchild to this insanity," Rachael's guard speaks up.

Rachael opens her mouth to protest, but Jack hushes her. "Your mother is right. You can't even shift right now. Lia doesn't want you to get hurt any more than I do."

I nod my agreement and watch as she deflates. I love her for wanting to support me, but she has more than herself to think of right now. Jack takes her hand, leading her out of the room after some goodbye hugs, her guard close behind. The rest of us wait in for AJ's guard detail to show up.

"If all these guards are coming here, who is with my grandma?" I ask.

"Don't worry about her. She has her personal guard and is more than capable," AJ assures me.

The guards take their places in the guys' rooms. AJ stays inside my room, perched next to the door. If circumstances were different, I would be anxious about spending my first night with my mates, but there's nothing remotely romantic or sexy about having a guard watch our every moves.

I'm exhausted, so I take my pajamas into the bathroom, take a quick shower, and get ready for bed. I lie down, after letting everyone know they are welcome to sleep next to me, and fall asleep as soon as my head hits the pillow.

CHAPTER TWELVE

LIA

"Wake up, princess," AJ's gruff voice pulls me from my dream.

"What's going on?" I ask groggily.

"We have to get out of here," he says, his voice full of urgency.

We quickly crawl out of bed as AJ moves from the entryway to the closet door, he motions for us to gather in the walk-in closet before closing the door behind us, moving to the wall in front of us. He presses a panel I'd yet to notice, revealing a darkened corridor. The closet door opens and we jump in unison, turning to face this new intruder but find a trio of guards. AJ ushers us into the corridor with the guards following behind prepared for any attack. The damp and dark hallway feels confining in ways I'd never felt before.

"What's going on?" I hiss.

"Not now, princess," AJ shuts me down.

We walk through a maze of dark passages until we come to a dead end. The front guard gives a series of knocks and waits a moment. Someone knocks back in a different pattern then he opens the door.

We exit into Queen Calyope's dressing room. What in the hell are we doing here? The leopard queen rushes forward, guards move out of the way, and she wraps her arms around me.

"I'm so glad you're safe," she sobs in my hair.

"What is going on?" I ask again, my voice firmer.

"They didn't tell you?" She gives me a confused look.

"No." I shake my head.

"Come sit down," she says, pulling me forward to a bench.

I stare into Queen Calyope's eyes, watching as a new string of tears build and spill forth. I feel her breathing slow as if she is trying to gain her composure.

"Please," I beg softly. "Whatever it is... just tell me." My mind flashes to Rachael then to Jack. "I know deep in my bones, something bad has happened. She nods her head slowly before releasing a final breath.

"There's been an attack," she begins. "The information the guards obtained indicated that it would be on Kenton, but..." she let the words trail off.

"Just tell me already," the words come out harsher than I intend but I can't take the suspense any longer. I need to know.

"It wasn't Kenton the attack was planned for... it was your grandmother, Queen Adrielle." I jerk my hands from hers.

"Is she all right? Take me to her now," I demand making my way to the door. AJ steps in front of me blocking the exit.

"Lia," Queen Calyope's voice calls out behind me but I don't turn, can't turn, because I know before the next words leave her mouth what they will be, what she will say. "Lia," her voice softer, closer than before. I fight the tears building in my eyes, blurring the stoic visage of AJ before spilling down my cheeks. Queen Calyope steps into my view taking my hands in hers once more. "I'm so sorry, sweet girl. I'm so sorry." I let the dam break and the tears pour forth as she pulls me into her arms.

The grief is overwhelming. Wave after wave pounding over me, never giving me a moment's relief to surface and breathe. I watched as her face appears in my mind, the moments we shared a movie reel playing in my head. She had brought me in, protected me, loved me, shared with me the memories of my mother, a woman that gave her own life to save mine. My only connection to my mother, to my history, gone... taken from me in an act of malice. I pull back from Queen Calyope, the wave receding to the flames of fire that began to burn deep in my belly.

"I want to know who did this," the venom coating my words. "I want to know who did this, because by all that is holy on this island, they will die by my hand." I charge for the door, but AJ tackles me, pinning me to the floor. I fight against him to no avail.

"You need to calm down, princess." His voice is gruff, and as the rage clears from my eyes, I can see there are emotions battling in his own. He's just as hurt by this as I am, and I can't help but wonder. Why? "If you go in there angry and grieving, you'll only get yourself killed."

I let the anger leave me as he helps me from the ground, turning back to face Queen Calyope. "Who's responsible?" I ask again, gaining my composure. I look behind her to my mates, their faces a mix of anger and sadness.

"We believe that Queen Rani was able to get to Adrielle's steward," Queen Sierra, the tiger queen, speaks as she enters the room from another hidden door.

"How do we know for sure it was my mother?" Kenton asks, emotions warring on his face.

"The steward admitted to it as soon as the guard grabbed him. Queen Rani gave him the poison he slipped into her tea.

We've detained more of Queen Rani's personal detail and they are being interrogated at the moment," AJ explains.

"Then how do we take her down?" I ask.

"With the information brought back from her beta, who took you, and this, it will be enough to strip her power and arrest her," AJ responds.

"Then do it!" I scream at him, trying to keep the anger and grief from returning.

"We need to stay strong." Kylah growls, and I agree. There will be time to grieve later. I let Rachael and Jack envelope me in a strong hug as my mates gathered around, joining in. I wanted so badly to let go, to let the tears flow freely, but I refuse to do so. With my grandmother gone, I am the only panther royal left, and I plan on doing everything in my power to make my grandmother proud.

"She will pay," I assure Kylah. I use the anger and resolve to pull me back. Everyone releasing me and allowing me room to breathe and move. I glance around the room taking in the surrounding faces. My grandmother may have been my last living relative, but my family was much bigger than just her. Now, I would do whatever was necessary to make sure they stayed protected.

"Tell me what to do next," my eyes landing on Queen Calyope and Sierra. A slow smile pulls across each of their mouths and I know that justice will be mine.

"The guards are rounding up the rest of her detail and husbands as we speak. As soon as most of them are accounted for, AJ and his crew will take her and place her under arrest. We will have a trial and determine her fate. Since Queen Adrielle is gone, you will sit in her place as the only other panther royal," the tiger queen explains.

"How long will that take?" I ask, eager to get it over with.

"The arrest will happen tonight, but the trial won't be

until after Queen Adrielle is laid to rest. That's more important to the clan," Queen Calyope takes my hand.

"Will you tell them how she died?" I sniff, trying to hold back the fresh set of tears threatening to fall.

"Of course. We need everyone to know of Queen Rani's treason. It will make the trial and sentencing easier to swallow. This has never happened before in our clan," she explains.

AJ tilts his head, as if listening to something. "It's go time," he says, motioning for his group to join him.

Half of the guards occupying the room filter out into the dressing room, making the room feel much larger than before. The adrenaline rush to my body is wearing off, and I can feel my legs shake beneath me. Kenton is the first one to my side, his arm snaking around my waist to help steady me on my feet. I look to him and can see the emotions affecting him; his brow is drawn forward and although he gives a smile, it falls short. I stop moving, turning into his body, and wrapping my arms around his waist. He squeezes me tight.

"I love you, Trouble, and I'll never let anyone hurt you. I don't care who they are. You're my family, today, tomorrow, forever."

I allow the tear to slide down my cheek. I know how hard this is for him, how those emotions are eating him alive on the inside. I could feel it with every fiber of my body, but he stood here being strong for me, reassuring me that'd he'd always be here to protect me, to love me, when... the funny part is... I didn't need his reassurance because I knew he would with every fiber of my soul.

"I love you too," I reply, gazing into his eyes. "... today, tomorrow, forever. What are you guys thinking? You grew up with Kenton's mom," I sob, realizing this has to be hard for him.

"She sealed her fate when she attacked my mate. I just feel

bad for my dads," Kenton growls, though he bunches his face in pain. The others chime in, agreeing with what he says.

"It's ok to be upset and angry. She is your mother. Even though she's done horrible things," I meet his eyes, trying to be sympathetic, even though I want to watch the bitch burn.

"You're too nice, Lia," Dom growls as he stands up and walks off.

I move to follow him, but Spence stops me. "Let him walk it off. He won't leave the suite."

I can sense their feelings, but mine are so strong they are getting all jumbled together. Fear, grief, anger, confusion are all mixing, making my head spin. With everything going on, I think my brain has overloaded. I close my eyes and drift off in the darkness.

CHAPTER THIRTEEN

DOM

Everything is just so fucked up. Lia is better, but now one queen is dead and another one will soon be as well. I don't think she understands what she has to do at this trial. She's too kind to sentence another person to death. Sure, she's strong enough, but I worry it will change something in her. Her big heart is something I can't lose.

I had to walk away. Queen Rani… She's always been cold, but I never thought she was capable of such horrendous acts. She was a loving mother, and I let myself trust her.

I'm so angry at myself for not seeing what she really is. I can't believe she would do this to her own son's mate and then her fellow queen. Is she the true leader of the Radicals? Or is this something else? My mind is spinning. I don't think I can be there for Lia the way she needs me to.

The queen's funeral will be hard on her, but I don't think I can stand to go. I'm already flashing back to my own parents' death. Why is everything always so messed up? I just want to go home, crawl in my bed, and not look back. But my brothers and my mate need me.

I'm already so broken and now she will know how

unworthy I am to be a part of her pack. I'm pacing back and forth in the hallway to the queen's other living quarters when Vance finds me. I meet his eyes and see my pain reflected.

"Want to talk about it?" he asks, sitting with his back leaned against the wall.

"No," I growl then pause. "Do you?"

He nods his head. Well crap. I sigh and plop down next to him.

"I can't stop thinking about my mom," he whispers. "How did everything go sideways so fast?"

"I don't know." I deflate.

"Lia's stronger than you think," he says, looking at me with an intensity he rarely shows.

"She's going to find out I'm too broken to love," I whisper my biggest fear out loud.

"Naw man. Chicks dig broken. She'll just try to put you back together," he gives a half-hearted grin and bumps my shoulder with his.

His comment is so unexpected it earns a full belly laugh from me. I needed that!

"Is that why you stormed off?" Vance asks.

"Partly. It's just hard to think I let myself trust someone who has done such…" I trail off.

"I know. I'm struggling with that too. I'm worried about Kenton. How will he feel once Lia has to order his own mother's death?" Vance asks.

"I hadn't even thought of that," I scrub my hands down my face. "This really will tear us apart, won't it?"

"Only if we let it. I stand by my mate and my brothers no matter what," Vance says, his voice growing hard. "The bitch queen has it coming. She tried to kill Lia and then killed another queen. It doesn't matter whose mom she is, she brought it on herself."

"You're right. Hopefully, Kenton can see it that way," I

sigh, my energy running on empty now. "I'm ready to go back."

"Sounds good. Lia is asleep again," Vance tells me as we stand up and make our way back to the living area.

The rest of our group is lounged out on the sectional, with Lia curled up in the corner fast asleep.

"You ok?" Spence asks, looking me up and down.

"Ok as I can be," I shrug, plopping on the couch next to him.

We sit in silence, no one's ready to discuss what's going on. Talking to Vance helped more than I had imagined. He's the only one who could understand my current state of mind. His mom dying the way she did… I don't know how I made it through her funeral, I think I was more worried about my brother. Maybe I can focus my feelings like that for my mate.

AJ steps out of the dressing room and all of our heads turn to find out what's going on.

"We got her. She's raving mad, but in a holding cell with double the guards," he announces.

"Very well. Have someone bring pillows and blankets for the kids. They will stay here until we can be sure there are no more snakes in the castle," Queen Calyope orders.

AJ motions and a few of the guards take off. I'm not sure how Lia is sleeping, but I can't imagine my mind settling down long enough to escape myself.

Looking around, I notice how tired everyone looks and agree; it would probably be a good idea to at least try. Things will not get any easier any time soon.

The guards return with stacks of pillows and blankets. I jump up and grab one then cover Lia. I grab another and lie on the floor next to the couch. I want to be close when she wakes up. Kenton sprawls out next to her, and the rest find places on the couch and floor.

"I do have bedrooms," Queen Calyope says, shaking her head with a small smile.

"We don't want to wake up Lia again," Vance says, and the queen smiles back at him.

"Young love." She shakes her head with a smile before walking out of the room.

I close my eyes and try to still my mind. Before I know it, exhaustion takes over me and I fall into the darkness I thought unobtainable.

I wake up with a crick in my neck and stretch, trying to release the tension. The sun streams through the window, pin pricks of light overloading my sight. The sounds of soft snores fill the air around me, and it takes a moment for me to realize where I am. In those brief moments, the events of last night had been nothing more than a bad dream. But it was worse than that, I had awakened to a living nightmare. Deceit, betrayal, and murder are now a part of my life. A fresh wave of grief washes over me. I try to stand quietly without waking Kenton, who snores quietly next to me, but my feet hit something soft and I hear groan.

Crap, I didn't see Dom lying there.

"Sorry," I whisper at him.

"It's ok. How are you this morning?" He stares at me, his dark eyes piercing right through me.

"I don't know. Is that a real answer?" I ask, my thoughts so jumbled I can't explain them.

"It's an honest one," he replies, sitting up.

"Wake up you lazy sacks," Dom hollers, shooting me a grin.

I give him a dirty look. "I was trying not to wake anyone up." I put my hands on my hips.

"I know, but they also would be irritated you let them sleep." He shrugs.

Everyone but Spence stirs. He apparently is a heavy sleeper. Dom stands up, walks over to him, and slaps his ass hard. Spence bolts up off the couch, causing the rest of the guys to laugh at him.

"What's going on?" he asks, confused.

"Nothing, Lia's awake," Vance says, still laughing.

"Oh," he replies, rubbing his backside. "Did you guys tell her?"

"Tell me what?" My heart pounds, has there been another attack?

"They arrested Queen Rani and her people," Dom replies, his jaw ticking.

"Good," I reply, not knowing what else to say at the moment. I have so many thoughts running through my head, but I don't want to hurt Kenton any more than I need to.

"I need food," Kenton groans before standing up and stumbling into the kitchen.

I follow him to see if there's anything easy to cook. Then remember we are in another queen's living quarters. Is it ok for us to help ourselves?

"Wait, shouldn't we get permission before we dig for food?" I ask.

"Why? She told us to stay here and I'm hungry," Kenton replies, giving me a strange look.

"But this is her home," I say, looking around.

"Trouble, the castle stocks everyone's kitchens, so she can replace whatever we eat. They don't want us leaving so I'm sure she already knows we will eat," he explains gently.

"Oh… I didn't look at it like that," I say, feeling dumb.

"It's ok; now what do we want to eat?" he asks as he opens the fridge.

I look over his shoulder. "Let's make French toast."

"Sounds good. Reid! Get in here and help me cook," he calls then turns and looks at me. "Go sit down. We got this."

"Fine," I roll my eyes but give him a small smile.

I join the others on the large couch, sitting between Spence and Dom. Spence throws an arm around my shoulder, and I lean into him enjoying the closeness.

We sit there in silence for a while, and I enjoy the peaceful interlude. I don't think we will get many moments like this with the storm that's coming. Rachael and Jack join us, followed shortly by Queen Calyope and her three mates.

"Good, you guys are making breakfast," she claps her hands together. "I hope you remembered to make enough for us."

"Of course," Kenton smiles at her, handing her the first plate.

I get up and go to the table. The guys pass out the food, placing another platter in the middle. I dig in loving the taste.

"This tastes sooo good. What did you do?" I ask between bites.

"Added real vanilla," Reid winks at me.

We finish eating then Queen Calyope pulls me aside. "I'm sorry to do this, but we have to plan Adrielle's funeral. Since you're her closest relative, you have legal authority," she gives me a sad look.

"I understand, but can you help me? You've known her for longer…" I try not to choke up.

"I can help. AJ will take you back to your room so you can get dressed then we will go to the lawyer's office first," she hugs me.

We walk through the hallway this time, instead of the secret passage. Several guards flank us, and one follows each guy into their room. I grab clothes and rush into the bath-room as soon as I get to mine.

I spend longer standing under the spray of water than needed, trying to delay the inevitable. I can't decide if I should go alone with the queen or take the others with me for support. What is considered normal in these situations? I need to be strong, to be seen as a potential leader if I have to sit in my grandma's seat for Queen Rani's trial, but right now I feel as strong as a newborn kitten.

As I finish washing up, I decide. I need to stand on my own two feet for now. I can come home and break down and let my guys catch me later. I'll go alone just to prove to myself I can do this. They can't help me at the trial so this will be good practice.

I emerge from the bathroom, straighten my spine, and tell AJ I'm ready to go. He says something quietly then motions for me to follow him.

"We're meeting the queen at the front doors," he explains.

"Don't grab the guys. I want to go alone," I tell him as he opens the front door.

"Are you sure?" he gives me a strange look.

"I'm sure. I need to work on making decisions on my own," I meet his eyes.

"Ok, princess. You better tell them. We overwork my guys as it is," he replies.

We knock on each door and once they are together, I explain to them I need to do this on my own.

"No, you don't. You can still be strong with support," Kenton protests.

"You won't be able to support me during the trial. This is something I need to prove to myself I can do," I explain.

"But," he starts.

"If she says she needs to do this alone, we need to respect her," Dom cuts him off.

"Fine, but I think you're just being stubborn, Trouble," he stares at me with a scowl.

"Maybe, but thank you for wanting to be there for me. It means more than you know," I kiss his cheek.

"We need to go," AJ cuts in.

"I'll see you all when we get back," I say, then follow AJ down the hall.

We make our way to the front of the castle, anxiety building in my chest.

"We can do this. I'm still with you," Kylah reminds me.

"I know. We are strong, we are survivors, and we just take this one step at a time," I say back, more for myself.

"Now you understand," she replies, her voice full of approval.

The leopard queen is waiting for us when we arrive. I follow her out to a waiting limo, and we drive into town to the lawyer's office.

"One decision at a time," she reminds me. "If we're lucky, her will, will spell out what she wants done for her funeral."

"That would make it easier. I didn't get a chance to know her that well," I admit, a single tear slipping down my cheek.

"Just know that she loved you as soon as she learned of your existence. She often talked of this summer and getting to know the woman you're becoming," Queen Calyope replies.

"I wish we would have gotten that chance. I was growing to love her as well," I sniff before taking a deep breath. Be strong Lia, you got this, I remind myself.

We spend the rest of the ride in silence.

CHAPTER FIFTEEN

LIA

The car comes to a stop in front of a modest, red brick building at the end of Main Street. The wooden sign hanging across the top, Coons and Sons Law Firm. I take a deep breath as I follow Calyope out of the limo. The weight of an entire clan now resting on my shoulders. I hadn't had enough time with her. Time to learn what I need to be even half the queen she'd been. So many rules, policies, politics, and etiquette I have yet to learn. I hesitate at the entrance of the building, an overwhelming smell of sandalwood rushing to my nostrils. AJ gives me a slight nudge and I continue into the office. There's an older lady sitting at the receptionist desk, her deep brown eyes protected by the overly large, round lenses of her glasses.

"Good morning," she remarks at our entrance. "Mr. Coon is already waiting for you." She stands and leads us down a narrow hall to the office at the end.

We walk past her through the door and see a tall, white-haired man sitting behind a massive dark wood desk. His office is paneled in dark wood, and the chairs are a buttery colored leather.

"Please sit. I'm sorry for your loss. Queen Adrielle was an amazing ruler, and I'm glad to have known her personally," he says as we enter, the guards staying outside the door.

"Thank you for seeing us so quickly," Queen Calyope replies as we sit down.

"Anything for the queens," he says, grabbing a stack of paper on his desk.

I'm not sure how this works, so I sit back quietly and observe.

"You must be Amelia. It's nice to meet you, though I wish it were under happier circumstances," he offers his hand over the desk.

I take it, shaking it briefly. "Likewise."

"Last week Queen Adrielle came in and updated her will to include this letter for you, Amelia," he says handing me a thick envelope with a wax seal on the back.

My heart catches in my chest. I didn't know what to expect, but this wasn't it.

"So now I will read her will aloud, since Queen Calyope is here as a witness," he looks at me, so I nod my head.

"Go ahead," Queen Calyope agrees.

The lawyer sits up straight, clears his throat and begins reading. "This is the last will and testament of Adrielle Huntsman. In the event of my death, I would like to be buried next to my daughter and husbands who passed before me. You can celebrate my life however you see fit, but please don't mourn for me. I've lived a long, full life and death is but another journey."

I sniff at this last line; the lawyer pauses for me to collect myself.

He continues. "To my granddaughter Amelia, I leave all of my earthly possessions that do not belong to the crown, though I'm positive you will be a queen in your own right someday, if you are not already."

"That's all?" I ask when he stops speaking.

"Queen Adrielle said it's enough. She's leaving everything to you, so she didn't really need any more formalities," the lawyer explains.

"Thank you for your time," I tell him, holding the letter she wrote me to my chest. I'm almost scared to read it. "Is it ok if I want to wait to read this until I'm alone?" I ask.

"Of course. My only job was to make sure it made it to your possession in the event of her passing," he says sympathetically.

"Thank you again, Mr. Coon," Queen Calyope stands.

I rise to my feet and follow her out of the office, our guard joining us, and back into the limo.

"Would you like to read your letter now or wait until after we visit the funeral home?" she asks me.

"I'll read it now. Maybe she says something about what she wants…" I trail off.

"Go ahead," the queen encourages me.

I crack the seal, open the letter, and begin reading.

My dearest Amelia,

I'm writing this letter in case of the event of my death, which I fear may happen sooner than either of us would like. I've seen signs of discord, little whispers that I hope is an old queen being paranoid. My study has all of my notes and journals, use these wisely sweet one.

In any case, if you are reading this, I'm so sorry that I'm no longer there with you. In the short time I've known you, I can already tell you will blossom into an amazing ruler in your own right. I see so much of myself in you and it makes my heart happy to know you are alive to carry on our family's legacy.

I know life will be hard for you. With the prophecy and the Radicals out there, how can it be anything else? But I will always be watching over you. Everything I have is now yours.

Please live, don't sink down into a pit of grief. I lived that way for much longer than I'd like to admit, and I don't wish that fate on anyone. I'm with the rest of my family now, so go out and enjoy the family you are building. It's ok to be happy, it is not disrespecting my memory, and don't let anyone tell you otherwise.

With Love,

Adrielle Huntsman

Wiping the tears from my eyes, I feel like my heart has broken into a million pieces after reading the words she penned in her own hand. She is asking the impossible, and I'm sure she knows it, but I will try to take her words to heart. How do you celebrate someone's life without missing them?

"I don't think she wants a traditional funeral," I say aloud.

"What would you do?" Queen Calyope asks me.

"I think we should have a service where everyone shares their fondest memories of her then a dinner in celebration of her life. She doesn't want people being sad, though that's impossible. So, we can at least make it as positive as possible," I reply.

"I think that's a lovely idea. Her favorite color was purple. We could ask that everyone wear purple instead of black. I think she would have loved that," she suggests.

"I love that idea," I agree with her.

We pull up in front of the funeral home. I take a deep breath before we enter then sit with the director and pick out all the little details. By the time we finish planning everything, I'm exhausted. In three days' time, we will celebrate the life of my grandmother then we will have to move on to a trial.

As we ride back to the castle, my grandmother's words weigh heavily on my mind.

"What happens after the trial? Do I continue to stand in?

When are the next trials for choosing the new queens?" I ask, the questions flooding out of my mouth.

"Normally the trials wouldn't be held for a few more years, but with Queen Rani going to trial and…" she gives me a sad look. "We will have to move the trials up to replace them."

"What does that mean for me? I'm the only panther royal left," I question.

"Even so, if you can't complete the tasks and prove your worth, the panther throne will sit vacant," she explains. "But I have every faith that you'll succeed. If the prophecy is true, you might be the one to replace us all."

We ride the rest of the way in silence, my head spinning with so many thoughts, but I can't seem to grasp ahold of a single one. By the time we return to the castle, I'm numb. Everything has been so overwhelming; I think my emotions checked out. AJ meets me at the door and leads us back to Queen Calyope's suit where he informs us the others are all waiting.

"Is it still not safe to be in our own rooms?" I ask him.

"Not until after the trial. Once Queen Rani has been found guilty, anyone that has aligned with her will attempt to run. We will stay vigilant, so we make sure we have caught everyone," he explains.

"I would think her being arrested would scare most of them off," I sigh. I appreciate them looking out for my safety, but I wouldn't mind having my own space.

"Don't worry, I've had rooms put together for you in my quarters, though the guys will have to share. Your stuff is being moved over as we speak," Queen Calyope informs me. "I want you to feel at home. Like it or not girly, you are family now."

She nudges me with her shoulder, earning a small forced

smile. I wish I could give her a real one but still can't bring myself to feel anything.

"Is it ok if I lie down for a little bit? I just feel over-whelmed," I ask her.

"Of course. When you're ready, we can start going through Queen Adrielle's things," she offers with a concerned look.

"I think I would like to do that soon, while I'm still… I guess the word is numb," I reply.

She nods her head and we walk the rest of the way back in silence. As soon as we open the door to her suite, the guys surround me.

"Are you ok?" Kenton asks.

"Do you need anything?" Reid looks at me.

"You're smothering her," Dom growls.

They stop and look at him and back up a little. "Sorry Lia." Spence gives me a sheepish smile.

"It's ok. I'm just overwhelmed right now. I need to go lie down, but you guys can join me," I offer.

The queen leads me to the room she has set up for me. I barely look around before flopping back onto the bed and closing my eyes. I can feel the guys looking at me, waiting to hear everything that happened. I hand them the letter as I fill them in on the lawyer's office and funeral home.

"I just feel numb right now and exhausted. I just want to turn off and lay here for a while," I explain.

"We can do that," Vance says, lying down next to me.

"We're good at lying around," Spence agrees. "I mean we are cats."

"This is true," I agree as the rest pile on the bed.

We relax for a while, but sleep escapes me. I keep thinking over her letter, and how she knew things were going on in the castle. Should I be worried about the other queens? I really don't want Rachael or Ava to lose their mothers. I groan and force myself to sit up.

"What happened to lying around, Killer?" Spence asks.

"I feel like there's a puzzle piece missing, and it's bugging me," I admit. "I think I need to let AJ read my grandma's letter."

"If you're sure," Reid drawls.

"I'm sure. I have nagging thoughts that the other queens aren't safe," I explain.

"Let's go find AJ then," Vance says, standing up.

We all get up and exit the room, finding AJ standing in the living area, next to the door.

"Sir, um I think you need to read my grandma's letter. Something about it is bugging me," I say, feeling uncomfortable sharing, but compelled to do so at the same time.

"First off, I'm not a sir. Second, that's a very personal thing, are you sure?" he asks, looking at me intently.

"I think you need to, at least the first part. Maybe you can make some sense of it," I reply.

"Hand it over then," he sighs, holding out his rough calloused hand.

I give him the letter, chewing on my bottom lip as he reads, his eyes darkening.

"Damn stubborn old lady," he roars, handing me the letter back. "Not to speak ill of the dead, but if she would have said something…"

"Well?" I ask, not knowing what to say.

"Sorry princess. I forgot myself for a moment," he collects himself.

"Don't apologize. She was a stubborn woman and she should have said something," I agree with him.

"Do you feel up to going through her study? I hate to ask, but we aren't permitted to go through your personal effects without you present," AJ questions me.

"We can do that," I intone. The last heart to heart we had here in the castle was in that room.

"Do you want us to come with you?" Dom asks.

"Yes. I think I'll need all the support I have for this," I answer honestly.

91

CHAPTER SIXTEEN

LIA

Our group heads to the study, a pit in my stomach growing larger with every step. This room will represent my grandmother to me more than anywhere else.

AJ hands me a key when we approach the door. I put it in the lock, my heart pounding against my chest. As I turn the key and open the door, the smell hits me, forcing a small sob from my throat. It smells just like her, a mix of jasmine and parchment.

"I'm sorry, princess," AJ gives me a sympathetic look.

"It needs to be done. Let's check her desk," I sigh, forcing my emotions down and focusing on the task at hand. I think I preferred the numb feeling over this ache in my chest.

I walk behind the large desk and sit in her chair. There's nothing laying on top of it and the drawers are all locked. She obviously didn't trust someone to keep them locked in a locked room.

"Does anyone know where she kept the key to her drawers?" I ask looking over at AJ.

He shakes his head no and I scrunch my mouth to the side as I think. If I were hiding a key where would I put it. I run my hands under the desk, looking for a hidden spot and find a button. I press it and the top drawer pops open. Bingo!

Looking in the drawer, all I find is some scrap paper and pens. That was a dead end. I get on my hands and knees under the desk, trying to see if there's another latch or button I've missed.

"Did you check the drawer for a false bottom?" AJ asks.

I poke my head out from under the desk. "What do you mean?"

"May I?" he points to the drawer.

"Be my guest," I wave at it then crawl out to watch.

He pulls the drawer all the way out and sits it on top of the desk then empties it of its contents. He taps on the bottom and then smiles. Grabbing a paperclip, he sticks it down next to the side of the drawer and lifts the bottom, hiding a secret compartment.

"How did you know that was there?" I ask, looking at him suspiciously. He found that too easily... Something isn't adding up.

"I didn't for sure, but it seemed like a good idea to check," he shrugs.

I look down in the drawer. It holds a key ring with several sized keys on it, and an old, battered journal. I take both out and motion for AJ to replace the false bottom.

Opening the journal, I start reading and gasp. It belonged to my mother. Tears stream down my face as I read the passage I opened to.

I met the man of my dreams, but I can't risk anyone knowing he's my mate. We've talked about running off together, but I'm not sure if it will work. What if they hunt us down?

Poor woman was fearing for her mate? Why would it matter if people knew? I flip the page.

My period is late, so I took a pregnancy test and it came back positive. I can't risk them killing my baby so I'm leaving alone. I hope he understands. I'm not even going to tell him I'm pregnant, it's safer for the baby that way.

That's the last entry. Adrielle lied to me? She said she didn't even know I existed. Maybe she just assumed I didn't make it… I have such conflicting feelings running through my head I want to scream.

"She had this journal, so she had to have known I existed somewhere," I whisper out loud.

"What do you mean?" Kenton asks.

"This is my mother's journal. The last passage says she's pregnant and running off," I explain.

"If she was paranoid about someone in the castle, maybe she didn't want to put either of you in more danger by revealing she's known all this time. With the way they killed black panther babies, she probably decided it was better if she allowed you to grow up in a safer environment," Reid says.

"That makes sense, but who is 'them'? She doesn't mention the Radicals," I agree, pushing my thoughts away to deal with at another time. We are here for a reason.

I pick the keys up and try them in the next drawer down until I find the correct one and it turns. Opening the drawer, I find it full of files. I hand one to each of my guys and we go through them.

The first one I open has titles to cars, and a deed to a house in it. I close it and set it aside and grab the next, which is tax information. I don't think what we are looking for will be here. I let the guys continue to go through the files while I move on to the other side of the desk.

Unlocking and opening the top drawer, I find a stack of notebooks. I thumb through the top two and find nothing interesting, but the third one has what we are looking for.

Rani is sending her thugs out of the castle regularly.

Rani is killing Radicals without a trial behind our backs.

So that's who is behind killing them, but why? Kelly and Amy were going after me. Wasn't that in her best interest? She had her own people attack me.

Overheard staff talking about poison.

Random notes that get more detailed as time goes on.

Rani is insisting her guard be used at the school instead of the castles, thankfully she's overruled.

Staff whispering about strange things happening in the Lions' quarters. Maid overheard Rani saying she will be the only queen one day.

My steward is acting shifty. I think he's up to something.

Overheard steward recruiting Cali's and Sienna's stewards for a mission.

That was the last entry.

"All the stewards are in on it!" I exclaim after reading.

AJ gets on his headset and the guards burst into action. I want to get to Rachael and her mom, worried they are targets now that most of the guards are with us.

"Stay here," AJ says, stopping me. "We've got this."

We wait, me pacing nervously back and forth. What if I realize all this too late? I hope everyone is ok.

AJ cocks his head before punching the wall.

"No!" I wail, praying it's not Queen Calyope.

"Who is it?" Reid asks tentatively.

"The tiger queen is unresponsive and her guard's missing," AJ growls.

"Queen Calyope?" I ask.

"She's safe and her steward in custody. They found him with a knife pacing outside of her office. Thankfully, the weasel is a coward," AJ growls.

I let out a sigh of relief but feel horrible for Ava and Marc. They will be scared to death.

"Gather the guards, the tiger family, and meet us back in

the leopard queen's suit," AJ yells. "Princess, you will help interrogate my guard. I can feel how dominant you are."

"I can do that," I reply then we head back to Queen Calyope's living quarters.

"Thank you for listening to your gut, princess," AJ says as we walk.

"If not, I'm not sure our leopard queen would still be with us," he glances sideways at me.

A thought occurs to me. "So are the guards for each queen the same kind of cat as her?" I ask.

"No, the castle guard is a mixed bunch from all the cat types, why?" AJ gives me a strange look.

"Was Queen Sierra's guard a lion?" I ask gently.

"Fuck!" AJ roars, the other guards wince and drop to their knees, for not being royal this guy is really dominant. "I should have pulled the lions until we could establish their loyalty, but I trusted my men. Hell, should we lock him up too?" AJ growls, pointing to Kenton.

"Hell no! You'll lock him up over my dead body," I growl back at him, getting ready to fight.

"That's what I'm trying to prevent," AJ sighs.

"Leave my mate out of it. He's mine," I stare at him, shocked he can hold my gaze.

We walk in a tense silence until we reach the leopard queen's suit. As we enter, the atmosphere is even more tense. I stick close to AJ to see what he needs me to do.

"Where are Conner, Kale, and Travon?" he asks, looking over the faces of his men.

"Missing," one guard shrugs.

He turns to the guards that have been accompanying us. "Go check on the prisoner guards."

"I think you have your answer already," I breathe.

"I believe you're right princess, but it never hurts to check. Let your cat out and demand to know who's loyal.

Kenton, Ava, and Queen Calyope, can you help, please?" AJ looks around.

The guards shift uncomfortably as the four of us call our cats to the surface.

"You got this Kylah?" I ask her.

"This will be fun," she purrs back.

AJ lines the guards up and we question one at a time. Going through the first three guards, everyone checks out. The next guard I step in front of starts sweating.

"Look at me," I demand, pushing my dominance at him.

"She'll kill my family. Please save them," he drops to his knees begging.

"What do you mean?" I ask.

"Queen Rani. She said she'll declare my family Radicals and have them executed without a trial if I don't report back what's going on," he snivels.

"Lock him up. You poor fool. If you would have talked to me, I could have prevented all this," AJ shakes his head.

"Just keep my family safe, please," the guard begs as he's dragged away.

As we work through the ranks, Ava finds one more guard with questionable loyalty, who is dragged away hastily. Looks like Queen Rani has her claws dug in everywhere.

"Little princess, only one of the missing was a lion. The others were all tigers," AJ points out once he dismissed the guards.

We all grab a quick dinner then I return to my room in the suite. I flop back and exhaustion overtakes me, falling asleep without bothering to change.

CHAPTER SEVENTEEN

HEATHCLIFF (SIR)

The news of the panther queen's death is disturbing. The funeral is soon, and I have a feeling my brother needs to know about this. I never much cared for Queen Rani, she was an extremist who skirted the rules, and rules were most definitely not made to be broken. Living as a lion in the noble class under her rule makes my skin crawl. Hopefully, the next lion is a better ruler than her.

I stroll through the empty hallways of the academy, trying to formulate the best way to approach Nathaniel. I have always wondered who could have been the mate he lost so long ago that had left him a shell of a man. I had my own opinions on the matter over time, but it wasn't until that panther princess showed up that I truly begin to wonder. The way he had stalked her when she was out there, during her class. I'd seen that territorial pace before.

I resolve to go speak to the stubborn lion. Making my way out to the field behind the school, I find him lying inside the shed I adapted for his home. Stubborn man has refused to shift back to human form for nearly seventeen years now.

"Nathaniel, Queen Adrielle has been murdered," I tell him.

The lion whips his head around and stares intently at me.

"It seems Queen Rani was bound and determined to take out her granddaughter, and when that plan was thwarted, she attacked the queens. The leopard queen was lucky...the tiger queen is in a coma of some sort." I explain to him.

Unexpectedly, I watch as his body ripples. He struggles, muscles contorting until finally, a shaggy, older version of my brother stands before me. His long black hair, a stark contrast to his pale blue eyes and skin that hasn't seen the sun in years.

"What do you mean her granddaughter," he croaks out, with a lot of effort.

"Welcome back, brother. I thought to never see you like this again," I reply, flabbergasted. He was feral... When did he regain his humanity?

"The girl," he growls.

"The panther princess that recently started here is the granddaughter of the now deceased panther queen. It seems she was given up at birth and adopted by a bear clan. When she shifted, we were alerted, and they retrieved her from that family and brought her to live here. While she was home to visit her adoptive parents, Queen Rani's lackeys kidnapped and poisoned her. She's since been arrested for her part in the kidnapping, attempted murder, and murder," I recount what I was told.

"But she's okay? The girl?" he asks insistently.

"She's physically fine, brother," I look at him strangely. Why is he so concerned with this girl?

"The prophecy. She has to fulfill the prophecy," he insists.

"Prophecies are rubbish," I shake my head.

"No, this one is real. All the witches have seen it," he insists, his voice becoming clearer each time he speaks.

"Whatever you say. Let's get you inside and cleaned up," I suggest. Being in his animal form for so long must have addled his mind. Witches and shifters don't mix, everyone knows that. I doubt he's even met a witch before.

"That's a good idea. I need to go to the funeral," he says, standing up stiffly.

"Does that mean you're staying with us?" I ask hesitantly. It's been so long since my baby brother has been around, I don't want to scare him off.

"For now, at least. I have a feeling I need to stick around," he replies and follows me back to my quarters.

CHAPTER EIGHTEEN

LIA

I zip up the bright purple dress I picked out for the funeral. It seems odd not wearing black, but fitting. I want to respect my grandmother's wishes the best I can. I hope the clan is okay with the funeral. They've all known her much longer than I have.

I step out in the hallway and run into Queen Calyope and her three husbands. They are all dressed in various shades of purples and it makes my heart soar.

"Thank you for everything," I throw my arms around the leopard queen.

"My pleasure. I really do consider you a second daughter, Amelia," she says, patting my back. "Are you ready for this?"

"As ready as I can be," I reply, pulling back.

The guys are waiting in the living room, each wearing shirts in the same purple as my dress. I smile when I see them, though it's bittersweet. I think Grandma would have loved seeing everyone dressed in purple for her. The guards are even wearing lavender shirts.

"Thank you all," I say sincerely, gazing around.

"Of course, princess. Queen Adrielle was much loved," AJ nods, his eyes glistening with unshed tears.

We start the procession to the chapel, anxiety building in my stomach with each step we take. How am I going to get through saying goodbye to the only blood relative I have left?

Dom grabs my hand squeezing it tightly. "We can do this," he says firmly. I'm not sure which one of us he's trying to convince.

"If you need to stay back…" I offer, just now realizing how hard this has to be for him.

"No. I'm here for you," he states firmly.

I squeeze his hand as a thank you. We reach the chapel, and I stop dead in my tracks. She's in there… I don't know if I can do this.

"The first step is the hardest," Vance puts a hand on my shoulder.

I nod, take a deep breath, and push the door open. The coffin is set on a large pedestal at the altar with the lid propped open.

"Am I supposed to go up to her?" I whisper.

"It's customary," Dom whispers back.

"Okay," I say, my voice shaky.

I slowly move forward, tears welling in my eyes. If I look at her, it makes it real. I'm not ready for this, but I can't stop it from happening. Halfway up the aisle I want to turn and run, but Dom keeps a firm hold on my hand.

"It's okay. Take a deep breath and keep walking," he whispers, squeezing my hand.

"I don't want it to be real," I reply.

"I know, but you need to do this. It hurts, but it's part of the healing," he eyes shine with unshed tears.

This is affecting him worse than I had imagined. I straighten up and take another step forward. If he can do this, so can I.

I arrive at the altar and take the steps up, standing next to her. They did her makeup just how she always wore it. Dressed in a royal purple dress, she looks like she's sleeping peacefully.

"Goodbye Grandmother. I wish we would have had more time together," I say then reach in and squeeze her hand.

"You did good," Dom whispers to me as we make our way to the front pew.

I nod and grab a tissue to dab my eyes that won't stop leaking. Now that we've been seated, the other royals pay their respects and join us at the front of the church, then the doors open to the public.

The church fills as the clan comes to pay their respects. My heart fills with pride as I see the sea of purple filling up the chapel. Once the last person is seated, the minister stands up and says a few words, then a procession of people stand up and tell stories of my lovely grandmother.

It's beautiful to hear all the happy stories people have of her, but it makes me sad that I don't have more of my own.

When the funeral portion is finally over, we wait until everyone clears out and fills up the dining room before we take our place at the head table. It feels backwards to the other meals we've had, but we wanted to this to feel more informal since it's a celebration of life.

"You're supposed to mingle before we eat," Kenton tells me, making my eyes grow wide. This will be the first time I've truly interacted with the clan.

"Kenton needs to stay up here. With news of what his mother has done, he's not safe," AJ steps in.

"That's understandable," I reply slowly. "Can the others come with me?"

"Of course, princess," AJ says, stepping back.

I give Kenton a quick hug before the rest of us make our way down into the crowd of people. I walk around, shaking hands, listening to how much everyone loved my grand-mother and how terrible it is she's gone.

"Amelia, my condolences," Sir grabs my hand in both of his. "She was a wonderful woman and will be missed by all."

"Thank you, Sir," I reply, noticing the man standing next to him.

He's taller than Sir, with the same long, jet black hair just hitting his shoulders. His piercing blue eyes stare at me intently, reminding me of someone, but I can't place it.

"Let me introduce you to my brother, Nathaniel." Sir opens his arm towards the man.

His brother? That means he's the lion from the school. I thought he refused to shift back to human. I glance over at the guys who are wearing the same shocked expression I feel on my face.

"Nice to meet you," I hold out my hand.

He takes it tentatively and I watch as the same smile grows on his face that I've witnessed for years in the mirror. No way!

"You look just like your mother," he whispers, just holding my hand, not letting go.

"Did you know my mother well?" I ask, wondering if he's possibly...

"She was my mate," he stares at me for a reaction. Sir lets out an audible gasp, but quickly regains his composure, showing no emotion. I'm beginning to think the man is a robot.

My eyes widen. But that means... "Are you my father?" I ask, my heart pounding out of my chest.

"I believe so. Nice to meet you Amelia," he replies, giving me a tentative smile.

"I have so many questions..." I trail off unable to organize my jumbled thoughts.

"As do I, but for now, duty calls." He points around.

I nod dumbly as Spence pulls me away. We walk around for a while more, shaking hands and listening to everyone's condolences. Grandmother's funeral dinner seems to go well, but I'm having a hard time staying focused. I can't believe I just met my birth father. I look around, monitoring Nathaniel. Every time I lay eyes on him, he's watching me as if I'm the most entertaining thing in the room. I guess for him, maybe I am.

We go back up to the head tables and join Kenton. It's so strange sitting up here with so many queens missing. I hope Queen Sierra will be ok. AJ says she's in a coma, but they aren't sure what's causing it.

They bring food out and the guards taste it before we can eat. The rest of the meal flies by, just a blur. I don't know how to react, and my feelings are all over the place. One thing is for sure, I need to talk to Nathaniel and learn everything I can about him and my birth mother. I have so many questions.

"Thank you, Grandmother," I whisper, Kenton giving me a strange look. I feel like somehow she gave me this gift from beyond the grave.

"I'll explain later," I tell him.

As the night winds down, people filter out, a heaviness sinks in on my heart. We've well and truly said our goodbyes, which means the trial is next.

The guards finish clearing the dining room and we get up to leave. I look out to see if I spot Nathaniel, but it appears they were ushered out as well.

"Wait! I need to talk to someone," I stare at AJ.

"Who is it and I'll send someone to find them," he says.

"Heathcliff and Nathaniel," Reid supplies.

AJ gives him a strange look before talking over his com. "Nathaniel hasn't been human for almost two decades," AJ says when he's finished.

"He is now. I met him tonight," I reply, not wanting to speak the connection out loud yet.

He tilts his head. "They've found them. We'll meet them at the panther study," AJ says as he leads us out of the dining hall.

I wish he would have picked a different place, but for now I guess it makes sense. I have to take over my grandmother's position temporarily at least, so I guess it's my study now.

I mull questions over in my head as we walk. Why did you give me up? Why didn't he talk to me when he saw me at the academy? What was my mom like? Does he know what actually happened to her? Wait, didn't it say his mate died overseas in Sir's notes?

We reach the study, and I take a deep breath before walking in. I sit on the couch and wait for Nathaniel to arrive.

AJ is pacing nervously along the far wall, which strikes me as odd. He's normally so calm, cool, and collected. His face is etched with worry. What has him so rattled? Did he and Nathaniel have issues in the past? They are around the same age.

The door opens and Nathaniel walks through followed by Sir. AJ falls to his knees at the sight of him. What in the world is going on here?

"Thank you for meeting with me," I stand up and meet the men.

"The pleasure is truly mine, Amelia," Nathaniel opens his arms as if he wants to hug me then drops them awkwardly while Sir stands as still as a statue in the doorway observing the room.

"Come sit down and let's chat," I point to the couch, a small pang in my heart when this reminds me of the first time I talked with my grandmother. "I have so many questions, but I don't know where to start."

"How about I tell you my story then you tell me yours?" he offers.

"Can I stay for this heart to heart? I'd very much like to know the story you've been avoiding since you shifted," Sir says from the doorway.

"I'm okay with it if he is," I shrug. I'm sure he's been worried about his brother for years. Why else would he let him live as a lion on academy grounds?

"Grab a seat brother, and anyone else who's staying," he looks around, his eyes meeting AJ's then his face lights up with recognition, before morphing into a look of suspicion.

"Who are you?" Nathaniel asks him.

"That's AJ, my guard," I answer for him.

"No, he's covered in magic," Nathaniel stands up, his skin rippling.

"Don't shift here brother. AJ has done nothing but protect Amelia," Sir steps forward, placing a hand on his brother's shoulder.

"Nathaniel," AJ stands, his voice full of sorrow.

"No! What the hell is this!" Nathaniel roars.

AJ reaches in his pocket, a single tear falling from his eye. He pulls out a vial of a thick purple liquid and downs it. His body shimmers and shrinks, morphing forms before a blonde woman who looks like an older version of me takes the place of AJ.

"Nathaniel, let me explain," she says, dropping to her knees in front of him.

"But you're dead! I felt you die at the same time Celene did," he roars, throwing himself away from her.

"I had to make everyone think I was dead if I was going to protect the panthers," she cries, her shoulders shaking with her sobs.

"Are you truly here? Are you really my Demetria?" he asks, falling to his knees and lifting her chin.

He stares at her face for a moment before wrapping his arms around her and crushing her to his chest. I stand there watching them with my mouth gaping open in shock. AJ is my mother? How? My head is spinning, emotions flashing through me at an alarming rate. I'm angry. How could she be so close to her own mother and not say anything? How could she not tell me? The pure shock of the situation takes back over, and I let them have a bit before interrupting.

"So… does anyone want to let the rest of us know what in the hell just happened?" I ask, staring at the two with wide eyes. My parents are both alive?

"Amelia," Demetria cries out and rises to her feet then rushes forward and wraps me in my arms. "I've wanted to do this so many times."

I pat the strange woman on the back, still in too much shock to do much else.

CONTINUE on with Lia's story in Prophecy

First of all, thank you for coming on this journey with me. When I started Lia's series it was a fun project for the teenagers in my life. I'm so thrilled to see how many people have fell in love with her story as well! Sorry about that little bomb at the end. Who would have thought? Book four will be coming soon.

For updates on releases check out my Facebook group. **facebook.com/groups/RosesReverie**

ABOUT THE AUTHOR

Rose lives in the Midwest with her husband, kids and two Great Danes. She enjoys crafting in her free time and watching movies with her family.

Sign up for our Newsletter get a free story
Rose Alexander Author Page
Rose's Reverie - Readers Group
Rose Alexander - Instagram
Rose Alexander Twitter
Rose Alexander Pinterest
Academy of Broken Dreams Reader's Group (Co-writes)